"You're forgetting something," he said

Lexie stared coldly at Rome Lockwood. "I've seen you to your door; isn't that enough?" she demanded.

His arrogant brow arched to mock her. "The good-night kiss. It's compulsory."

"Oh, God." She exhaled an angry breath. "Do you honestly think for one minute that I'm going to kiss you? This whole evening has been a farce, but this is one laugh you're not going to get."

Rome shrugged. "It's a difficult thing to carry out. I quite understand why you wouldn't want to do it."

She glared at his handsome, mocking face, then succumbed to his blackmail. Her breath caught when her lips touched his firmly molded mouth.

"Not bad," Rome murmured appraisingly. "Now let me show you how it's done...."

JANET DAILEY AMERICANA

Every novel in this collection is your passport to a romantic tour of the United States through time-honored favorites by America's First Lady of romance fiction. Each of the fifty novels is set in a different state, researched by Janet and her husband, Bill. For the Daileys it was an odyssey of discovery. For you, it's the journey of a lifetime.

The state flower depicted on the cover of this book is mayflower.

Janet Dailey Americana

ALABAMA—Dangerous Masquerade
ALASKA—Northern Magic
ARIZONA—Sonora Sundown
ARKANSAS—Valley of the Vapours
CALIFORNIA—Fire and Ice
COLORADO—After the Storm
CONNECTICUT—Difficult Decision
DELAWARE—The Matchmakers
FLORIDA—Southern Nights
GEORGIA—Night of the Cotillion
HAWAII—Kona Winds
IDAHO—The Travelling Kind
ILLINOIS—A Lyon's Share
INDIANA—The Indy Man
IOWA—The Homeplace
KANSAS—The Mating Season
KENTUCKY—Bluegrass King
LOUISIANA—The Bride of the Delta Queen
MAINE—Summer Mahogany
MARYLAND—Bed of Grass
MASSACHUSETTS—That Boston Man
MICHIGAN—Enemy in Camp

THAT BOSTON MAN

Harlequin Books

TORONTO • NEW YORK • LONDON
AMSTERDAM • PARIS • SYDNEY • HAMBURG
STOCKHOLM • ATHENS • TOKYO • MILAN

Janet Dailey Americana edition published April 1987
ISBN 373-89821-5

Harlequin Presents edition published February 1980
Second printing February 1982

Original hardcover edition published in 1979
by Mills & Boon Limited

CHAPTER ONE

THE DIN OF THE NEWSPAPER OFFICE was steady; telephones ringing, the clatter of typewriters and voices, an unceasing hum of activity. Sitting on the edge of a desk in an area partitioned away from the rest of the staff workers in the room, Lexie Templeton was impervious to the background noises. A paper cup of black coffee was in one hand and a half-finished Danish pastry in the other.

Her attention was on her co-worker Ginger Franksen, who was also her roommate and friend. Lexie veiled the amusement that glittered in her blue eyes as she thought, not for the first time, that Ginger seemed the epitome of the fresh, innocent Midwestern type, which she was. Two years older than Ginger's twenty-two, Lexie felt at times like Ginger's mother instead of a friend, and at other times simply irritated by Ginger's traditional outlook.

She studied the slim, blue-jeaned figure of her roommate pacing about the alcove, long and beautiful corn-silk hair flowing past her shoulders. There was little makeup to detract from Ginger's wholesomely attractive features, that all-American look of pure honey that gathered men like bees. Ginger rattled on in a troubled and despairing voice with a quaint Midwestern accent, but it was her words that were making Lexie lose her taste for the pastry in her hand.

A sideways glance caught the amused but tolerant look of the third member of the impromptu gathering. Shari Sullivan, whose desk Lexie was sitting on, was considerably older than both of the others, but she was hardly the mother figure of the group. Sophisticated, chic, always dressed to the teeth, Shari was a blonde, too, thanks to the expert skill of Boston's best and most sought-after hairdresser.

Despite all Shari's worldly airs and hard-bitten glamor, Lexie often felt sorry for the woman. She so obviously clung to the image of youth while seeking status and prestige with greedy hands.

They were definitely an incongruous threesome. Lexie had often wondered what inner needs the three of them fulfilled in each other. Obviously there was something; they congregated each day at Shari's private desk for morning coffee, Ginger coming from her lowly position in the sports department and Lexie from her fast-riding post in political news. Shari had *the* society and gossip column in Boston.

"...and Bob was so angry because I wasn't in when he called last night." Ginger continued her lament that had been going on for the past several minutes.

Lexie wrapped a paper napkin around the rest of her Danish pastry and tossed it into the waste basket beside the desk. "I suppose you apologized for going out to do your laundry," she commented dryly.

"Well, I was sorry that I wasn't there when he called," Ginger defended.

"Honestly, Ginger—" exasperation riddled Lexie's response "—how can you let yourself become a door-mat for that man?"

"I am not a doormat," came the protest. "He wanted to talk to me and I wanted to talk to him. We just didn't make the connection, that's all. But that has nothing to do with my problem. What Bob is really upset about is this weekend. I can't make up my mind whether I should go with him to Cape Cod or not, and I'm afraid if I don't go, he'll ask somebody else."

"Let him," Lexie declared in disgust. "Bob Jeffers is a sexist and you'd be well rid of him. He wants you at his beck and call—never vice versa."

"I think you hate men, Lexie," Shari observed in a husky, cultured voice she had cultivated to perfection over the years.

"I like men well enough," Lexie said, denying the allegation, "if I can find any that will really treat me like an equal. You should have been with me yesterday when I interviewed that new candidate for Congress and heard him explain why he didn't have any women holding the responsible positions in his campaign. He gave that old song and dance about the difficulties of a single woman traveling in the company of so many men and problems of a married woman leaving her husband and family behind while she's on the campaign trail." Lexie stared angrily at the black liquid in her cup. "Why is it that a man is never asked how he manages to combine marriage and a career successfully, but a woman always gets that question thrown at her?"

"Excellent point," the older woman agreed with a throaty laugh.

"And speaking of careers—" Lexie warmed to her subject with a vengeance "—stop and think about the way men have taken over. Women always did the cooking until men discovered they could make money at it.

Voilà! Now they're chefs. The same is true with sewing and clothes. Men found out there was money in that and now our fashion designers are almost exclusively male. The same holds true with hairdressers. It used to be a woman's job, but men are making a fortune at it now. The list just goes on and on and on."

"It's a pity we can't convince them they can make money having babies," Shari offered in a dryly amused voice.

"Isn't it, though?" Lexie murmured, impatiently brushing a lock of titian hair from her forehead. "No matter what men say, secretly they want a woman to assume the traditional role of wife and mother and helpmate."

"I don't think that's true," Ginger inserted.

"Believe me, it is." Lexie's head bobbed with positive certainty. "A man may tell you that he feels a woman should work if she wants to, but what he really means is some other woman—not his wife. Men are such shallow creatures. They want women to soothe their furrowed brows, to pander to their insatiable male egos, to tell them what great lovers they are, and the women's reward is the so-called pleasure of their company." Her gaze strayed to the tear sheet on Shari's desk top, a photograph of a man dominating the page. "And he's the worst of the lot," Lexie accused.

"Rome Lockwood!" Shari exclaimed in disbelief, false eyelashes intensifying her round-eyed look.

The grainy newspaper photograph didn't do the man justice, but Lexie had seen him too many times in person to be deceived by the picture. She had never met him personally, only observed him at political functions. That had been enough to form her opinion.

Lean, dark features were molded into a stunningly handsome male face. Jet black hair grew with rakish carelessness above the wide intelligent forehead. Equally dark eyes glittered from the paper, a knowing light in their depths as if he knew the power of his attraction. And that mouth caught by the photograph in a disarming smile. . . . More than once Lexie had seen it work its charm, smoothly and subtly and successfully.

"Yes, Rome Lockwood," she repeated. "God, that name sounds like something Hollywood would make up!"

"He isn't a politician," Shari remarked, "So how did you come to meet him?"

"Political functions often become social functions," Lexie answered, again with a trace of contempt. "And, as you know, no social function is considered a success unless Rome Lockwood attends. Have you ever seen him with the same woman twice in a row?"

Shari thought for a moment. "I can't say that I have—not twice in a row. No one has even come close to hooking him yet, although a lot have tried— desperately. Which is probably why his black book has so many names. He probably finds safety in numbers."

"If I were Rome Lockwood, I'd be worried," Lexie observed.

"Why?" Ginger walked to the desk to look at the photograph claiming the others' attention. A glimpse of the man in the picture made her add, "With looks like that, he'll never have to worry about the supply running out."

"He should worry that some of his many women might get together and compare notes. I'm sure he finds safety in numbers because it conceals the fact that he isn't man enough to keep one woman satisfied.''

Her caustic statement was initially greeted by silence, then Shari released a short, stunned laugh and reached for a scratch pad and pencil. "That's priceless, Lexie!" she declared. "May I quote that in my column?"

Lexie hesitated, then shrugged diffidently. "I don't care."

Shari hurriedly wrote it down, rings cluttering her fingers and long nails polished in a fashionably gaudy purple red. "The whole town will be buzzing when they read this. Everybody will be talking about my column," she murmured aloud, smiling with feline satisfaction when she read what she had written.

"I think that's a horrible thing for you to say," Ginger accused. "You're probably just jealous, Lexie, because you aren't one of the girls he takes out."

"You're way off base." Lexie gave a pitying look to her roommate. "I'm not the least bit jealous. All his good looks and charm can't change the kind of man he is. And I know his type. There'll never be just one woman in his life. He's always going to have to prove what a man he is by stringing out a long line of conquests. The disgusting thing is that all the other men look up to him, envy him. They refer to him as a man's man. It's what they would all like to be."

"A lot of women agree," Shari pointed out.

"A lot of women are fools," Lexie replied. "They cherish fantasies that they'll be the one to catch him."

"And why not?" Shari argued. "He's tall, dark and handsome, not to mention wealthy."

"And he's a born Casanova." Lexie drained her coffee and tossed the cup in the wastebasket with an air of finality.

"And you're a born cynic," Shari smiled.

"I prefer it to being a born innocent," she retorted, straightening from the desk and glancing at her wristwatch. "I'd better be getting back to my desk. Stan is bound to be wanting me by now," she said, referring to her editor.

"I'd better go, too," Ginger stated. "See you later, Shari." She followed Lexie as she left the thinly partitioned alcove. "Neither one of you said what you thought I should do about this weekend. Should I go with Bob?"

"I can't tell you whether or not you should go," Lexie frowned. "It's your decision, Ginger, not mine."

"I don't feel right about going," the girl sighed, flicking her long, straight blonde hair away from her collar.

"Then don't go."

"But if I don't, Bob won't ask me out anymore."

"If that's the kind of guy he is, then you're better off without him."

"That's easy for you to say, but I don't want to get the reputation of being a prude."

Meaning that Lexie had. But it didn't bother Lexie at all. The ones who called her that were the ones she wouldn't have dated if they were the last men on earth. They were the ones who fell into the general category headed by the likes of Rome Lockwood.

With the striking combination of copper red hair and startling blue eyes, Lexie didn't lack for invitations to go out. Thus, she had her choice of companions, and she chose those whose company she would enjoy and not have to fight off. A few times her choice had proved to be wrong, with her idea of a good time and her date's idea clashing.

"With an attitude like that, Ginger," Lexie offered as they reached the hallway where they would separate to go to their different departments, "you could wind up with the reputation of being easy. And that can lead to a lot more heartbreak than being called a prude."

Ginger looked skeptical, but didn't argue. "I'm meeting Bob after work, so I'll see you later on tonight at the apartment."

"What about supper?"

"Don't get anything for me."

Lexie's desk was barely distinguishable from the rows of others just like it. The typewriter, files and clutter of papers on top of it half-covered the standard black telephone. The file cabinet, desk and typewriter table fenced in her chair. As Lexie squeezed through the gap between the typewriter and the short file cabinet, the man at the desk facing hers glanced up. Ralph Polasky was a staff reporter twenty years her senior, and inclined to laziness.

"You're back," he observed. "Mike was here a minute ago looking for you."

Lexie had expected her absence from the desk to be noted. Very little escaped Mike Farragut's attention. The little wheels on her chair legs squeaked as she pulled it away from the desk.

"What did he want?"

Her co-worker shrugged. "Just asked where you were. I told him I thought you'd gone for some coffee."

"I can imagine his reaction to that," she murmured dryly.

Ralph Polasky smiled. "You know Mike. He went off grumbling about women, coffee and gossip."

"And, of course, you agreed with him," Lexie accused him jokingly.

"Of course," her fellow reporter grinned.

"Chauvinist," she taunted and drew the expected laugh.

The phone rang at his desk. He answered it, then cupped a hand over the mouthpiece. "I forgot. I think Mike left something on your desk," he said, then resumed his conversation with the telephone caller.

Sitting down, Lexie quickly skimmed through the papers scattered haphazardly over her desk top. One practically leaped from among the others, demanding her attention. It was the story she had just written and turned in to Mike not more than an hour ago. She sighed when she saw what was left of it after Mike's ruthless pencil had gone over it. She leaned back in her chair and began reading through the changes and corrections.

After reworking the story, she submitted it to her editor again. Mike read it through and nodded his approval. Words of praise were the last things Lexie expected from him, and she didn't receive any. But the announcement that he was giving her a by-line on the story was ample reward.

The following afternoon, as she was leaving for the day, she passed Ralph Polasky in the hall. He'd been out on assignment all day and was just coming in to write up the story.

"What are you trying to do?" was his greeting. "Make a name for yourself?"

She laughed, guessing he had seen the story with her

by-line in the morning edition of the newspaper. "Jealous?" she teased. The elevator doors were just closing, and Lexie hurried to beat them. "Don't work too hard, Ralph," she mocked as she slipped inside the elevator.

The good mood didn't last long. Her roommate Ginger was at their apartment when Lexie arrived home. She was still in the thralls of indecision about spending the weekend with her boyfriend, Bob. Lexie simply couldn't sympathize with her roommate's dilemma, but it was the only subject Ginger wanted to talk about. She discussed it fixing dinner, after dinner, and while washing the dinner dishes. By then, Lexie's patience had worn out and she exploded.

"I don't care what you do, Ginger!" Her hands were on her hips, a damp dishtowel clamped in her fingers. "Either make up your mind or shut up! I'm tired of hearing about it!"

Her roommate's guileless face was incapable of concealing anything. The hurt expression that Lexie had inflicted transformed Ginger's and tears glistened in her eyes. The expression on Ginger's face made Lexie think of a puppy that had just been scolded severely. Without uttering a sound, Ginger turned from the sink and dashed to her bedroom.

"Damn," Lexie breathed, and tossed the towel on the kitchen counter. She felt like an insensitive brute and was angry for feeling guilty at speaking the truth.

Ginger remained in her bedroom for the rest of the evening. Twice Lexie walked to the door to apologize and make peace. Each time she was kept from knocking by the realization that Ginger was indulging in a childish sulk and by the feeling that she had been in the right to demand that Ginger make up her mind.

The next morning Lexie was dressed and walking out the door when Ginger finally came out of her bedroom. Lexie paused wondering whether she should make a comment about the previous night or let the matter rest.

Finally she chose the middle ground. "The coffee is made. I'll see you at work," she said as she walked out the door.

She didn't see Ginger again until midmorning, when she glanced up to find her roommate standing in front of her desk. Rouge had been applied to pale cheeks with a heavy hand, and Ginger's eyes seemed unnaturally bright.

"I've decided that I'm going to Cape Cod with Bob this weekend. I thought you'd like to know." Ginger's announcement had a defensive, almost challenging, ring to it.

"Bob will be happy to hear that," was the only comment Lexie made.

Personally Lexie thought her roommate was making a big mistake, but she kept it to herself. Ginger was already aware that she didn't like Bob. There was no need for Lexie to voice her disapproval and put more of a strain on their relationship.

"What time will you be off work tonight?" Ginger asked after a second's hesitation. "I thought I'd fix a pizza."

"That sounds good," Lexie replied, accepting the peace offering. "I don't think I'll be late. I'll let you know if it looks like I will be."

"Okay. Talk to you later." Ginger walked away, her mouth curving into a fragile smile at the truce she had achieved.

With a sigh, Lexie turned back to her typewriter. There were some girls who simply had to learn the truth about certain men the hard way, and Ginger was one of them, she decided. Luckily she hadn't. She'd known about it since childhood.

"There you are, Lexie." Shari Sullivan's familiar voice interrupted Lexie's thoughts. "Just the person I was looking for."

She glanced up in surprise. Although she often stopped by Shari's office, the older woman rarely, if ever, came to hers. Lexie had always suspected that it was a case of status. When a person had their own column, less established reporters were to call on them and not the other way around.

"You were looking for me?" She said with some curiosity.

"Yes, I was." Shari glanced over Lexie's shoulder to read the partially written story in her typewriter. "Do you have a few minutes or are you under a deadline for this piece?"

"I almost have it wrapped up. I can spare a few minutes," Lexie said. "What is it?"

"Your comment about Rome Lockwood created quite a sensation." Shrewd eyes steadily held Lexie's puzzled look.

"My comment?" Lexie repeated.

"The one I quoted in my column the other day about Rome Lockwood not being man enough to keep one woman satisfied," Shari reminded her.

It had completely slipped Lexie's mind. "Oh, yes," she said, nodding. "I'm glad for you that you got a lot of response from your readers."

"Believe me, I did, honey." A faintly smug smile

curved the scarlet mouth. "I was at a cocktail party last night and everyone was murmuring about it. The remark was positively fantastic. It titillated everyone's interest."

"You said it would."

"Mmm, yes." Shari dismissed that as being too obvious to warrant a comment, "What I need now is another quote like that to keep generating the interest."

"You mean, from me?" Lexie laughed faintly. "I'm sorry. I wish I had a ready supply of them at my fingertips, but that one came strictly out of the blue."

"Surely you can come up with another," the blonde coaxed.

"Honestly, I wish I could, but bright quips just aren't my line." She shook her head apologetically, half-amused by Shari's persistence.

The columnist wasn't deterred. Sitting in the straight-backed chair beside Lexie's desk, she took out a pencil and notepad from her oversized handbag.

"I won't give up so quickly. Rome Lockwood is news any time and when people mention his name, they're going to mention my column in the same breath," Shari insisted with the tenacity of a bulldog. "Tell me something about the women he's seen with," she prompted.

There was a helpless shrug of her shoulders as Lexie tried to comply. "I don't know anything about them. They're just your usual assortment of your wealthier society girls, jet-setters, Bryn Mawr graduates and all that, with an occasional model thrown in to add color."

"Why do you think he's so popular? Why is he regarded as such a catch?"

"You said it yourself. He's handsome and rich and

single. Of course, without the money, he wouldn't be as sought after as he is," Lexie qualified.

"Without money, what would he seem to you?" Sharie questioned.

"The modern-day equivalent of a gigolo, probably," she answered, and Shari's pencil flashed across the paper.

"He's regarded by many as an excellent business-man." Shari glanced up from her jottings.

"Really? All he does is manage the family's hold-ings. His father made all the money. The only thing Rome Lockwood has to do is spend it," Lexie returned caustically.

"I'm told that he's very astute about making invest-ments," Shari appeared to argue with the assertion.

"No doubt you were told that by the businesses Rome Lockwood has invested in. They aren't the ones to accuse him of making unwise investments, are they?"

"Being a feminist as well as a political reporter, what do you think his views are regarding women's libera-tion and equal opportunity?"

Lexie couldn't resist smiling at the question. "I'm sure he believes in equal opportunity. Although I imagine his version of it is that he'll go out with a blonde, brunette or redhead." Her telephone rang and Lexie missed the flashing smile of satisfaction from Shari as she answered it. "This is Lexie Templeton."

The classily dressed blonde rose from her chair, say-ing to Lexie in a pseudo whisper, "Thanks a lot. See you later." With a wave of a be-ringed hand, Shari left her to take the phone call in private.

If it hadn't been for one of the other staff members,

Lexie wouldn't have known that Shari had quoted anything of their conversation in her column. She was one of those newspaper reporters who never reads the newspaper. But her comments regarding Rome Lockwood were printed, meted out as tidbits over the following ten days, thus ensuring Shari of daily readers anxious to see if she said anything about Rome Lockwood.

After a few days Lexie's comments about the man became a source of gossip even within the newspaper. A few members of the staff thought she was going too far, but mostly the reaction was just good-natured ribbing that Lexie took in stride.

The little café next to the building housing the newspaper office was crowded when Lexie entered it a little past noon. There were a lot of familiar faces among the diners since its nearness made it the logical luncheon place for reporters.

"Hey, Lexie!" one of the reporters who usually worked the police beat called. "What's the latest word about Rome Lockwood?"

She just smiled and shook her head, redgold curls dancing about her neck. "You'll have to read Shari's column and find out for yourself, Hank. I'm not going to give you any exclusive."

The others at his table laughed and began talking among themselves. Lexie's attention had already been diverted back to her original problem, finding an empty chair in the crowded restaurant. Then she saw a man motioning her to join him—Gary Dunbar, a feature writer for the paper and a quiet man she had dated and lunched with often in the past. She made her way across the room to his table and the empty chair opposite his.

"I was about to decide I'd have to order a sandwich to go and take it back to the office." Lexie slid into the chair with a grateful smile. "Thanks for letting me join you."

He half rose politely out of his chair as she sat down. A lock of baby-fine brown hair fell across his brow and he self-consciously pushed it back into place. There was a gentle strength in his tanned yet faintly ruddy features and Lexie was suddenly reminded of how much she liked him.

"I was going to stop by your desk to see if you were free for lunch," Gary said.

The waitress stopped, handed Lexie a menu, and automatically filled the cup in front of her with coffee before hurrying on. "It's probably a good thing that you didn't," Lexie replied, opening the menu to glance at the list of food she almost knew by heart. "I was tied up on the telphone. If you'd waited for me, we wouldn't have found a place to sit."

"It's usually full during the lunch hours," he agreed.

A plate of hamburger and fries was set in front of him and the busy waitress turned to take Lexie's order. "I'll have a bacon and tomato sandwich, no lettuce, butter instead of mayonnaise, on white bread not toasted," she requested. With a curt nod, the woman was gone and Lexie returned her attention to Gary. "Go ahead and eat," she prompted. "Heaven only knows how long my order will be in the kitchen, and there's no sense in letting your food get cold."

Gary hesitated, then reluctantly began to eat his sandwich. Between bites, he said, "You're really creating quite a stir around town."

"You mean about Lockwood?" She sipped at her coffee.

"You're being pretty hard on the guy, aren't you?"

"I just call it the way I see it," Lexie shrugged, indifferent to the vague criticism in his words, then smiled, "Besides, it sells newspapers."

"And makes a name for Shari Sullivan, who already possesses an inflated sense of her own importance to journalism," he remarked.

"She works hard at her career and has for some time." As far as Lexie was concerned, she was stating a fact and not defending her friend. "She's earned the right to some recognition." A plate was set in front of her by a rushing waitress. "Just a minute," Lexie called her back and returned the plate with its sandwich. "I don't want the bread toasted."

The waitress accepted it with a grimace of impatience and a look that said Lexie was being fussy.

"Do you know, I've never had the nerve to do that?" said Gary, a wry smile tugging at the corners of his mouth.

"Do you mean, send food back when it wasn't the way you ordered it?" Lexie questioned.

"I never have," he admitted.

"As long as I'm buying the meal, I'm going to get what I pay for," she declared firmly.

"You should."

Within minutes, the sandwich was set before her, this time made the way she had requested it. By that time Gary was finished with his meal, but he had another cup of coffee while Lexie had her lunch.

"What's on your agenda this afternoon?" he asked.

"I have to go straight from here back to the office to

write up the Senator's press conference held this morning," she answered. "Nothing new—just the usual promises. He's coming up for re-election. How about you?"

"I have an interview at one-thirty with a woman who's being hailed as the new Grandma Moses. She's eighty years old and sounds like a character," Gary explained. "I talked to her on the phone. She seemed more full of life than I am at one-third her age."

"Does she live here in Boston?" Lexie had finished her sandwich and was sipping at a fresh cup of black coffee.

"No, in Concord."

Her eyes rounded into sapphire nuggets. "It's nearly one now. You'll be late if you don't hurry."

He glanced at his watch in surprise, irritation thinning his mouth. "I lost track of the time."

Both luncheon checks were lying together on the small table. As Gary reached to pick them both up, Lexie tried to beat him to them.

"Don't worry about that, Gary," she insisted. "Lunch is on me today."

"No, I'm buying." Both checks were in his hand as he straightened from the table. "I invited you to join me, remember?"

"You've bought my lunch the last three times." She didn't mention that they had lunched alone only three times. "It's my turn—I'm a liberated lady. It's all right for me to buy a man's lunch."

"Not this man." Gary slipped a tip under his plate for the waitress.

Impatience with his attitude flashed through her. "You always told me that you treated women as equals."

"With certain exceptions," he joked, missing the warning glitter in her eyes. "One of them is letting a woman buy my meal."

"If that's the way you feel, we'll go Dutch," Lexie argued stubbornly.

"Lexie, I don't invite a girl to join me and then make her pay for her own lunch." His ruddy complexion was steadily darkening with embarrassment. "Come on, now. You're making a scene."

Compressing her lips tightly together, Lexie stifled the rejection she would have liked to make and managed a stiff and ungrateful, "Thank you for lunch, Gary."

"That's better." He winked and started toward the cash register. "Let's get together this weekend. I'll give you a call."

Lexie didn't respond. She wasn't absolutely sure that she would take his call when it came. This little episode had made a gigantic black mark in her mind against him, one that wouldn't be easily erased. Because Gary had just evinced a deep-seated belief in the double standard for men and women.

Never a drum-beater, Lexie was still very definitely a liberated woman. She simply didn't go around preaching of the inherent inequalities in modern-day society. It was incidents like this one that brought her feelings boiling to the top.

"Men," she muttered.

"You said it, honey," the waitress paused beside her table with a coffee pot in her hand. "More coffee?"

"No thanks."

"It seems like you can't live with a man and you can't live without one," the waitress commented.

"There are times when I think I could," Lexie stated. "Live without one, that is."

"A piece of advice from one working girl to another. If you can find someone to buy your lunch, don't argue, just hand him the check."

Lexie just smiled and nodded, but she could never do that. It went against the grain. Gary worked, too, and his budget was probably just as tight as hers. It was only stupid male pride and an equally stupid code of standards that kept him from letting her pay for his meal.

In theory, most men were all for equal rights for women. But practice.... The whole thing infuriated Lexie, but she had long ago learned to control her temper.

CHAPTER TWO

THE WHOLE LUNCHEON SCENE left a bad taste in her mouth. Lexie tried to push the memory to the back of her mind, but it kept drifting into her thoughts. Her inability to concentrate on the story she was writing rankled.

The notes in her tablet weren't stringing together into a story the way they normally did. In the last hour, since she had returned from lunch, she had spent more time staring at the typewriter and the notes, than putting words together to form sentences. It was disgusting and irritating.

"Would you tell me where I might find a Miss Alexandra Templeton?"

Lexie's desk was toward the front of the room and she heard the inquiry being made of one of the employees near the door. The male voice was vaguely familiar, but she couldn't place it. Sighing at the interruption, she turned in the chair to confront the visitor.

"Lexie!" the fellow employee called as she turned. "There's someone here to see you."

An amazing hush seemed to spread across the room. Lexie recognized the man walking toward her desk at about the same time that everyone else did, and the blood froze in her veins for one stunned second. She watched Rome Lockwood cover the distance between them with a curiously graceful economy of movement. There was a relaxed arrogance about him; he was tall and lean, exuding a male presence that drew every eye in the room.

Tension rippled through her. Lexie knew why he was here to see her. If she didn't, the hard black look of his gaze would have informed her that it wasn't a social call. When he stopped in front of her desk, no disarming smile was offered to alleviate the chiselled firmness of his mouth.

Lexie would have been less than honest if she didn't admit that the sight of this tall, dark exceptionally good-looking man stirred her pulse. But what was true for a man was true for a woman. You could be physically attracted to someone without liking him or what he represented.

As he towered in front of her desk, Lexie was aware of the raking scrutiny of his gaze, tearing her features apart from the curling thickness of her golden auburn hair to her smoothly sculptured chin. It left Lexie with the sensation that she had been dissected as analytically as a frog in a laboratory, thoroughly, without an organ missed.

"You are Miss Templeton?" he asked for her confirmation. The pitch of his low voice was controlled and even, as was his expression.

"Yes," she acknowledged with a brief nod.

"*This* Miss Templeton?" The latest edition of the paper tossed onto her desk, opened to Shari Sullivan's column.

"Yes, I am that Miss Templeton, Mr. Lockwood," she confirmed.

There was an indolent flick of one dark brow and a

measured glitter of amusement in the coal black depths of his gaze. "Then you do recognize me." Yet there was an underlying grimness to the straight line of his well-formed mouth.

"Of course." A ghost of a smile touched her lips. As if he really believed he was not instantly recognized wherever he went, she thought.

Her peripheral vision caught the approach of Mike Farragut, her assignment editor. He was a Hollywood image of a harried reporter, clothing rumpled, in need of a shave, a cigarette always in his hand, eyes squinting through smoke. Mike was coming to her rescue, or, more correctly, to the newspaper's rescue.

"Mr. Lockwood," Mike greeted him, switching his cigarette to his left hand to shake hands. "Is there anything I can do for you? Mike Farragut's the name."

"No, thank you. I merely wanted to speak to Miss Templeton," was the dangerously smooth reply.

"I see." Mike, too, was in no doubt about the subject Rome Lockwood wished to discuss with Lexie. He glanced at her pointedly, his squinting eyes asking her a different question from the one he voiced. "Are you free?"

The unfinished article in her typewriter gave Lexie an excuse, but she didn't choose to use it. Lexie felt no compunction to hide from this man. Granted, there was a rather intimidating aura of authority about Rome Lockwood, but he wasn't her employer.

"Yes, I can spare Mr. Lockwood a few minutes." Her tone was cool and deliberately condescending.

"Perhaps—" Mike's gaze swept the staff room, aware that the meeting between the two was the cynosure of all eyes and ears, regardless of the pretended interest elsewhere ''—you would care to use my office for your discussion,'' he suggested tactfully. ''It will afford you a bit more privacy.''

''That would be best. Don't you think so, Mr. Lockwood?'' Lexie challenged.

''Whatever you wish, Miss Templeton.'' The knowing glint in his eye seemed to mock her desire not to have an audience for their meeting, as if he anticipated she would come out second best.

That ruffled her fur, but Lexie concealed her feelings, rising from her chair to walk around the desk. Although tall herself, she still had to tip her head back slightly to look at Rome Lockwood.

At close quarters, she was also aware of how physically fit his leanly muscled frame was. There was a vague fluttering in the pit of her stomach. No man had a right to be so sexually attractive, she thought in irritation.

''This way, Mr. Lockwood.'' Lexie took the lead in showing him to Mike's private office. When the door was closed and they were isolated from the others, she turned to confront him. ''What exactly did you want to speak to me about?'' As if she didn't know.

''I'm curious, Miss Templeton.'' He appeared infuriatingly relaxed and in command. ''I don't recall meeting you before. Perhaps you could enlighten me where and when it was?''

Rome Lockwood remained just inside the room while Lexie walked leisurely to the front of Mike's desk and turned around, leaning backward against it and resting her hands on its top.

''We haven't met before,'' she informed him. ''I have seen you at several functions I have attended in the course of my position as a reporter, but we have never spoken to each other."

"We have never met before," he repeated. "Yet according to what you've said in the paper, you claim to be an authority on me."

"I have never claimed to know you personally Mr. Lockwood," Lexie corrected, "only your type."

"Which is—unless I've missed one of the columns—a chauvinistic, rich gigolo, minus any sense of fidelity, whose business skills are questionable. Did I miss anything?" He tipped his head sideways in challenge, half-closed eyes not veiling the sharpness of his gaze.

Listed that way, her remarks did seem to constitute an overly sweeping condemnation, but Lexie wasn't going to retract a word of it. "I believe that encompasses the bulk of it," she agreed.

"It's a very despicable type you've classified me in, wouldn't you say?"

"I'm sorry if you find my opinion objectionable, but there it is." It was worded as an apology, but it wasn't offered as such. It came out more like an ultimatum: take it or leave it.

"I do find it objectionable," Rome Lockwood stated, "because you don't know me, Miss Templeton."

"I don't care to know you. It's sufficient that I know of you," she retorted.

"Meanwhile, your opinion of my so-called type continues to be printed in a widely circulated newspaper." The grim set of handsomely sculptured features indicated his displeasure.

"I can't do anything about that," Lexie shrugged. "You'll have to speak to Miss Sullivan. She's the one who decides what goes into her column. I'm certain she would be more than willing to print any rebuttal you would care to make—''

"I have no intention of giving any credence to your comments by making a public response to them, Miss Templeton,'' Rome Lockwood interrupted sharply, the pose of calmness stripped away by the slashing cut of his cold anger.

"That's your decision to make.'' She remained calm, although that determined set of his jaw revealed a side of his character she had not thought existed. "If my comments are needling you, striking a little too close to home, you'll have to speak to Miss Sullivan. She prints them; I don't.''

"Your opinion doesn't bother me in the least,'' he stated. "I've been called worse by more erudite people than you. Unfortunately, there are members of my family who are hurt by the accusations you've made about me.''

"How selfless of you!'' Her honey-coated response revealed that Lexie didn't believe for an instant that Rome Lockwood was concerned about the feelings of others.

An unamused smile curved his mouth, a shadow of the charming look Lexie had seen him bestow on those he favoured with his presence. Still, she felt a fleeting wisp of its magic, compelling and entrancing. Luckily she had been graced with a built-in immunity almost from birth.

"It's a pity I can't return the compliment,'' Rome mocked, "and declare that you, too, are selfless.''

"As I said before, Mr. Lockwood—'' Lexie ignored his taunting comment "—if you have any complaints to make regarding the contents of Miss Sullivan's column, you'll have to take them up with the writer herself."

"I make it a rule never to deal with a middleman when I can go directly to the source," he stated.

"Middleperson," Lexie corrected.

"And you're Miss Sullivan's source," Rome continued with hardly a break.

"So what are you saying?" she challenged. "You want me to stop voicing my opinion or . . . what? You'll sue me or the paper or both for slander?"

"If I contemplated taking legal action, now or in the future, my attorney would be speaking to you now, not me."

Sighing, Lexie leaned more fully against the desk. "Then I'm afraid I don't understand what you're hoping to accomplish by seeing me."

"I had hoped," his voice was dry, "that I might be able to reason with you."

"Change my opinion of you, you mean." Laughter danced in the blue lights of her eyes, taunting him with the impossibility of the idea.

"Perhaps," he conceded. "At the very least, I wanted to set your facts straight regarding the allegations you've made about me."

"Which ones are those?" Lexie questioned, malicious satisfaction warming her blood. "Was it the comment I made about your money? You did inherit it from your parents, didn't you?"

"Yes."

"And your job—if it can be called that—consists of managing the family holdings, doesn't it?" she retorted.

"It can be more difficult to keep money than it is to make it, Miss Templeton," he stated, aware that her implication was that his job was an undemanding one.

"Why? Have you made some bad investments?" Lexie countered.

"Your comments have insinuated that I did."

"All I said was that some of the opinions that have been expressed might be coming from people you've invested money in, therefore their claims that you are remarkably astute in business matters could be prejudiced in your favor for their own self-preservation." Her eyes rounded with false innocence. "I can't be responsible for the interpretation someone else might make of the remark."

"Of course not," Rome agreed cynically. "You put all the right qualifying words in, didn't you? Might, some, could be. And you slide right off the hook." His narrowed gaze added "like a worm" and Lexie's fingers curled tightly around the edge of the desk top.

"I believe," she continued, trying to remain relaxed and not let his unspoken gibe tighten her voice, "that I also made a reference to your playboy image. There are too many witnesses for you to deny that you have a steady variety of dates."

"Because I'm not man enough to make one happy," he said, reminding Lexie of her comment.

Looking at him, he seemed all man and very familiar and expert at the ways of satisfying a woman. A coursing heat flamed through her body before Lexie could check it with the reminder that his image was false. She wasn't about to fall into the embarrassing trap of trying to defend that statement.

"You must admit that your stream of conquests has

been long and varied." She didn't change from her original theme.

"Assuming, of course, that I conquered them," Rome countered.

"Please, Mr. Lockwood—" Lexie forced out a disbelieving laugh "—don't try to give me that old story that they were all just good friends. Next you'll be trying to convince me that you're practicing celibacy, waiting for the right woman to come into your life."

"Is it so inconceivable?"

Lexie smiled with feline case. "Are you a virgin?"

There was a hint of a smile about his mouth and the darkening light of amusement in his eyes. "You come straight to the point, don't you?" he mused. "No. Are you?"

She hadn't expected him to parry her thrust with the same question, and momentarily, it disconcerted her. "You'll never find out the answer to that, Mr. Lockwood."

A wry smile quirked his mouth, not unattractively. "I forgot. With my chauvinistic tendencies, you're certain that I'll apply the double standard to your answer, believing that it's all right for a man, but not for a woman."

Lexie glanced away from him, not letting him bait her into an answer. "The truth is you've done more to perpetuate the male myth of superiority in Boston than James Bond ever did."

"With my 'equal opportunity' practices?" Rome mocked.

Her gaze flashed back to him. "Admit it. Your fragile ego couldn't take a really liberated woman. You're no different from any other man. It's all right for somebody else's wife to be liberated as long as it isn't your own."

"I wouldn't object in the least," he stated flatly.

"Really?" She was openly scornful and skeptical, her memory flitting back to lunchtime. "You mean it wouldn't be a blow to your manhood if a woman paid for your meal? Took you out for an evening?"

"I'm a gigolo, remember?" Rome recalled her words again. "Why would that bother me?"

"Would your pride allow the woman to be the bread-winner?" Lexie continued.

"Are you talking about equality or role-reversing?"

"They're one and the same thing," she retorted. "If a man and woman are equal, why does it matter who does what? Has a woman ever asked you out? I don't mean to her home for a party, but out for the evening—at her expense."

"No." He eyed her in a speculative fashion, vaguely withdrawn.

"And if she did?" she prompted knowingly.

"I would have no qualms about accepting the invitation," Rome insisted.

"Empty words," Lexie dismissed his answer, certain he was saying it only in an attempt to influence her in his favor. "Do you have any plans for Friday evening?"

He hesitated, considering her thoughtfully, before answering, "None that I recall."

She moved in for the kill. There was no doubt in her mind that Rome Lockwood hadn't meant what he said. "Will you go out with me on Friday evening?" Lexie challenged.

His dark gaze narrowed for a second. "I presume

that a man retains the same prerogative as a woman and can choose which invitations he wishes to accept and which he would rather refuse. Or is he expected to go out with whoever asks him?"

"Of course he has the prerogative." She had known all along that he would refuse to go out with her—from the very second she had thought of the idea. He would use the fact that she so heartily disliked him as an excuse for not wishing to spend an evening in her company, but she would prove her point just the same.

"You expect me to reject your offer, don't you?" His speculative look was unnerving, but Lexie kept silent, not answering his astute question. After a few seconds, he went on, "My first reaction was a flat no, but on second thoughts, I'll accept."

"You will?" Lexie breathed, trying to conceal her shock and dismay.

"Yes, I will." His alert gaze noted her reaction and he smiled in satisfaction, his eyes crinkling at the corners. "For the sake of experimentation and because I'm just as anxious as you are to prove a point."

"But you don't really want to go out with me," she protested impatiently.

"Are you chickening out, Miss Templeton?" Rome taunted. "Empty words? Would you like some salt and pepper for seasoning while you eat them?"

"No!" Lexie flashed.

"Then your invitation stands?"

"Yes!" she snapped.

"I repeat, I accept." He was so smooth and so sure of himself when he spoke that Lexie wanted to pick up the water cooler and dump it on his raven-black head. "What time will you pick me up?"

She had an uncomfortable moment when she thought about her car and its sad and aged state. It immediately became humorous as she imagined the suavely handsome Rome Lockwood sitting in the passenger seat as the car crow-hopped down the street.

Mustering all her poise, Lexie asked, "Will seven o'clock be convenient?"

"Yes."

"I'll pick you up at seven, then." Lexie straightened from the desk, suddenly anxious to be out of the room and away from him so she could gather her scattered wits and plan what she was going to do. "If you'll excuse me, it's time I was getting back to my desk."

As she started to brush past him to the door, he said quietly, "Would you like my address so you'll know where to pick me up?"

The crimson flush in her cheeks nearly matched the color of her hair as she retraced her steps to the desk for pencil and paper. "Would you write it down for me, please?" Lexie requested stiffly and handed the pen and paper to him.

Gleaming onyx eyes outlined by dark sooty lashes were laughing at her. It was a relief when they turned their attention to the paper while the hand guiding the pen made bold, slashing letters. Rome tore the paper with his address from the pad and handed it to Lexie.

"Don't lose it," he mocked.

She would have loved to put a match to it and destroy it, but that wouldn't alter the situation she was in, thanks to her rashness.

"I won't." She slipped the paper into her pocket and returned Mike's pencil and pad to his desk.

"You may find that a man's role is not quite as easy

as you women seem to think it is," Rome offered as she again started for the door.

"I doubt it," Lexie retorted. "Men are prone to exaggerate the importance of their role to assure themselves it is."

"Were you a born man-hater?" he inquired with a curiously amused look.

Lexie didn't know how he had meant the question, but she answered it seriously. "I don't hate all men— only certain types." Rome Lockwood had to know what category he was in.

Without waiting to hear whatever rejoinder he might want to make to that, Lexie opened the door leading to the staff room. The low, taunting chuckle that came from deep in Rome Lockwood's throat was a more grating response than anything he could have said.

Again they were the cynosure of all eyes when the newspaper staff saw that they had reappeared. For a short distance, her path to her desk and Rome's path to the exit were the same. Her expression was deliberately closed so the others would not see her less than successful outcome from the meeting, by her standards. Since she walked slightly ahead of Rome Lockwood, she didn't know if his triumph was apparent in the darkly lean features.

At the point where their paths diverged, Lexie quickened her steps while attempting to maintain her outward composure. Mike Farragut had commandeered her desk in return for his and stood at the sight of them. Lexie knew she would have to field a lot of probing questions from him—to satisfy his own curiosity as well as the company's interest in the outcome.

She was bracing herself for that when she heard

Rome say, in a voice that was unnecessarily clear and carried to the farthest corner of the hushed room, "Don't forget—this Friday evening at seven. I'm looking forward to our evening together with the greatest pleasure...Lexie." The use of her Christian name was done deliberately to suggest intimacy and Lexie seethed in silent indignation.

She turned and smiled sweetly, "I won't forget... Rome," her voice was equally low and projected just as far as his.

Rome seemed neither offended nor surprised by her quick adoption of his attitude. In fact, there was a distinct twitching around his mouth, as if he was controlling laughter. Lexie felt her temper nearing the boiling point, but he was already striding toward the exit door, out of range of her sputtering anger.

"Did I hear right?" Mike claimed her attention.

"You heard right," Lexie answered, her jaw clenching to keep her temper under control.

The cigarette between his fingers had gone out, the filtered end unable to burn, but Mike didn't notice there wasn't any smoke to squint through as his gaze bored into Lexie's profile.

"Maybe I didn't understand what I heard," he said. "Do you have a date with him on Friday?"

"Yes, I do." She was gritting her teeth so tightly that they hurt.

"I'll be damned," he muttered. Then louder, "I'll be gawddamned!" Mike started to laugh, a rollicking sound as he turned to the now intensely curious onlooking staff. "She's a witch," he declared to them, "a gawddamned, red-haired, genuine Salem witch! She's got Rome Lockwood eating out of her hand. She goes into my office with a man who was upset by all the things she was saying about him, and when they come out, she's got a date with him!''

"Why don't you put an announcement in the paper, Mike?'' Lexie grumbled, certain he was going to run down the halls shouting the news to everyone.

He put his arm around her shoulders and gave her a bone-crunching hug. "You deserve a bonus for this, Lexie. Rome Lockwood has some influential friends. We were all expecting some pressure to be applied to put an end to the way Shari has been bandying his name about with your insults. But you just wrapped him around your little finger.''

"It wasn't quite like that,'' she protested, both at his praise and the painful embrace.

Others had begun to gather around, bombarding her with questions, asking how she'd done it, what had she said.... It became impossible for Lexie to deny she had used feminine allure. Nobody believed her. Finally she just gave up and let the storm of enthusiasm rain over her.

In the midst of it all, Shari Sullivan appeared. "Honey, I just heard that Rome Lockwood was here to see you!'' she exclaimed. "What happened? Was there a big scene? What did he say?''

For the first time the others fell silent, eyes gleaming, giving Lexie a chance to tell her cohort of the triumph. "He indicated he wasn't pleased with the items that had been appearing in your column about him.''

"Hell! Get to the point!'' Mike barked. "She has a date with him this Friday.'' He couldn't wait any longer.

"What?'' Shari's poise slipped as she stared at Lexie in dumbfounded amazement. "Is that true?''

"Yes," Lexie nodded. It was impossible to explain with everyone telling what they thought the story was.

Finally the columnist shooed the others away and sat Lexie down in her chair. "I want you to tell me about it just the way it happened," she insisted, drawing up a second chair and leaning eagerly forward.

"I would rather forget the whole thing," Lexie protested, tension hammering at her temples.

"Don't be silly," Shari frowned impatiently. "This is going to make a terrific wrap-up for the story."

"Don't you dare print in your column that I'm going out with Rome Lockwood!" If it hadn't been for her other comments Shari had included, Lexie wouldn't be in her present fix.

"Why not?" The other woman bristled, then immediately changed to a reasoning attitude, appealing to Lexie's reporter instinct. "Just think of the lead-in. 'Feuding reporter and playboy out on the town—together!' It'll be sensational, honey."

"I don't care how sensational it is, you aren't going to print a word of it." Lexie held her ground.

"If I don't, one of the other papers will," Shari reminded her. "I've made you and Rome Lockwood news in this city. Someone will see you together. Why let someone else have the story?"

Shari's logic defeated Lexie. "Very well," she conceded, "but I don't want anything in there about the meeting today and what was said between us. And nothing about our date, other than that we were seen together."

"You can't be serious!"

"I am," said Lexie; this time nothing would budge her. "No one else will have that story. Only Rome

Lockwood and I are going to know what we said to each other, and that's the way it's going to stay."

"But the date.... Surely you can phone me some details Saturday morning so I can get it in Sunday's paper," Shari wheedled.

"Listen, Shari, the date is going to be a disaster."

"No date with Rome Lockwood is a disaster. It's more like a dream come true as far as half the woman in this town are concerned."

Lexie realized there wasn't any way she could trust the older woman with the true story of what happened. Shari's sole interest was in furthering her reputation. She couldn't be trusted to keep the actual circumstances that led to the date out of her column. Lexie didn't object to Shari's knowing, but she certainly didn't want it appearing in print.

"That's all you're going to get from me, Shari," Lexie stated. "You'd better be satisfied with that."

When further cajoling and pleading and reasoning didn't elicit more information from Lexie, Shari accused her of not being a true friend, an attack designed to make Lexie feel guilty, and left in a huff. Lexie sighed and turned back to the notes she had taken at the press conference that morning.

When she went home to her apartment that evening, Lexie thought she had left the furor of Rome Lockwood's visit behind her. But her roommate, Ginger, was waiting eagerly for her arrival, filled with questions about the rumors that had so swiftly circulated through the building.

"Yes, it's all true," Lexie nodded helplessly. "Rome Lockwood did stop by this afternoon. I did talk to him.

And I do have a date with him this Friday night. End of story."

"You really have a date with Rome Lockwood!" Ginger sat down in the nearest chair, long corn-silk hair swinging about her shoulders as she shook her head. "Lexie, you must be thrilled out of your mind!"

"Far from it." Lexie kicked off her shoes and sank into the only other easy chair in their small apartment. Wryly she noticed how the strain between Ginger and herself had been temporarily lifted—at least on Ginger's part—because of Rome Lockwood. The man's name seemed to be magic. Black magic was probably closer, Lexie decided.

"How can you be so down?" Ginger protested at Lexie's disgruntled air. "You should be jumping for joy. I would be."

"What about Bob?" Lexie wished she could bite off her tongue. She and Ginger had got along so well until Bob had come on the scene, so why had she brought him up?

"Bob is different," Ginger retorted defensively. "But Rome Lockwood.... Well, he's like a celebrity in a way. Who wouldn't be excited about that?"

"It depends a great deal on the circumstances."

"What aren't you telling me?" Ginger tipped her blonde head to one side in a frowning study of Lexie's grim look.

"That it isn't as wonderful and glorious as all of you are thinking it is. This date.... We trapped each other into it." She sighed heavily.

"What?" Ginger was confused.

"Rome was upset about the things in the column," Lexie began at the beginning. "We started going down the list of my quotes to show him my observations were accurate. When we came to the one about Women's Lib and equal opportunity, things got out of hand. Look—" she straightened in her chair and leaned forward "—if you tell this to Shari, I swear I'll move out of this place."

"What is it? I won't tell. I promise." Ginger crossed her heart in a child's promise, her eyes widening.

"At lunch today, Gary wouldn't let me pay for his lunch. It wasn't the manly thing to do and all that rubbish."

"What has that got to do with Rome Lockwood?" her roommate demanded.

"It was right after lunch that I talked to him and I was still upset by Gary's stupidly chauvinistic behavior. When Rome and I began talking about equal rights, I asked him if he would let a woman take him out for an evening and buy him dinner, et cetera. He said he wouldn't object and I challenged him to go out with me. He accepted, even though he despises me and I hate him. So that's your grand date that everyone is buzzing about."

"You're kidding!" Ginger breathed.

"I only wish I were." Lexie raked her fingers through the long titian curls of her hair and leaned back in the chair to stare at the ceiling. "I have to pick him up at his apartment at seven on Friday."

"Are you going to?"

"I have to," Lexie sighed, "I tried to back out of it when he first accepted. That's when he threw the challenge back to me. We're both trapped."

"Where are you going to take him?"

"I don't know." An impish smile curved her mouth.

"How does MacDonald's sound for dinner and a drive-in movie later on? Can't you just picture Rome Lockwood in my banged-up Mustang? He's so tall."

"Lexie, you wouldn't!" Ginger exclaimed in horror.

"Wouldn't I? I'd love to do just that. To tell you the truth, that's just about all I can afford." The grimace was back.

"I can lend you a few dollars," her roommate offered. "Haven't you got anything in savings at the bank?"

"There's my vacation fund," Lexie remembered.

"But you were saving to go to London."

"It looks as if I'll have to postpone the trip to London until next year," Lexie laughed briefly and without humor as she made the pun: "This year I'm going to spend it on Rome."

CHAPTER THREE

WITH THE EARRING FASTENED, Lexie stepped back to survey the results in the mirror. Shimmering coppery hair framed her oval face and cascaded in curls to her shoulders. Beneath the auburn wings of her brows she had added a touch of eye shadow, and on her mouth a lipstick of muted claret glistened on the shapely curves of her lips.

The jersy-like silk of her dress was silver gray, its style elegantly simple, clinging softly to her figure without molding it in a bold display. A necklace of antique silver circled her throat, its scrolling design studded with turquoise. Matching earrings dangled from her lobes, the blue of precious stones winking through the loose curls of her red hair.

Lexie touched a finger to the pulsing vein in her neck that betrayed the inner state of her nerves. She took a calming breath and tried to make herself relax. The tension didn't leave.

"Stunning!" Ginger exclaimed from the doorway. "Where did you get that dress, Lexie? I haven't seen it before."

"I bought it for the occasion." The dryness in her mouth coated her voice as she turned away from the mirror to pick up her matching shawl of silver gray. "I decided if I was going to splurge on this evening I might as well go all the way.''

"And the jewelry—I've never seen you wearing that necklace before.''

"A gift from my father.'' Lexie had kept it tucked away in the folds of her lingerie in a dresser drawer, but it had seemed appropriate to her to wear it tonight.

"Aren't you excited?'' Her roommate's innocently beautiful face was wide-eyed with imagined anticipation. "I know all about the circumstances, but aren't you just a little bit excited?''

"I'm dreading the entire affair,'' Lexie stated unequivocally as she picked up her evening bag. Pausing, she thought aloud, "I wonder if Rome Lockwood has ever been stood up.''

"You wouldn't!'' Ginger gasped.

"I wish I could,'' Lexie sighed wistfully and walked from her tiny bedroom, not much bigger than a large closet.

"Are you leaving now?'' Ginger followed.

"I have to if I want to be at his apartment by seven. I doubt if I'll be very late coming home tonight.''

"Bob said he'd call me tonight, so I may not be here.''

"See you in the morning, then,'' Lexie offered in goodbye.

"Have fun!'' Ginger wished her.

Lexie's mouth twisted wryly on that thought as she left the apartment. Her small car, freshly washed and shined, was parked outside of the aging apartment building. The interior of the Mustang was vacuumed and spotless. Except for the dented and rusting mudguard, Lexie thought it looked better than it had in months, not quite in Rome Lockwood's luxury class of transportation, though.

Nor did its appearance fit her extravagant plans for this evening, dinner at one of the poshest restaurants that Lexie knew about in Boston, followed by after-dinner drinks at an equally renowned club featuring live entertainment. It was going to be an expensive evening. Lexie freely admitted that she was doing it to impress Rome that a woman was just as capable of planning a lavish evening as a man.

The narrow, twisting streets of inner-city Boston didn't permit Lexie to drive fast. A taxi would have been better, but her already depleted finances wouldn't allow it. Turning a corner, she slowed the car as she neared the address Rome had given her.

Squeezing her car in a parking spot between a Mercedes and a Cadillac, Lexie switched off the engine. "It isn't the company you're used to keeping, is it?" she chided the cars, adding wryly, "Talk about the high-rent district."

It was a shock to discover that her legs felt weak when she stepped out of the car. Lexie silently wished the evening was already over. It soon would be, she consoled herself and squared her shoulders.

In front of his door, she punched its buzzer and waited. It felt strange to be standing outside a man's apartment, picking him up for a date, but Lexie wouldn't have admitted that for anything. When there was no answer, she pushed the bell again and waited.

It suddenly occurred to her that possibly Rome Lockwood had changed his mind. Anger flushed through her at all the effort she had gone to and the wretched anxiety of waiting for Friday to come. She had joked about standing him up only to have it happen to her. She started to spin away from the door when it opened. Her lightning-blue glance flicked sharply to the lean, dark man framed by the opening.

His hard male vitality seemed to reach out and ensnare her. A smile of apology that was forming on his disturbing mouth was arrested for a scant second as his gaze darkened mysteriously in a sweeping assessment of her.

There was something much too admiring about the look and it curled her toes with its sheer sensuality. It was a fleeting sensation, replaced by a formal polite expression as Rome opened the door wider to admit her.

"Come in," he invited.

Lexie hesitated, letting her pulse settle to an even pace before entering his apartment. She knew how sexually appealing Rome Lockwood was to women—to her—but she wasn't intimidated by it. Being forearmed, she knew she would not be so foolish as to take any attention he paid to her seriously.

She let her senses register his physically disturbing state. The white of his shirt, only half-buttoned, contrasted with the even bronze tan of his skin. There was a sheen of dampness to his jet dark hair, so invitingly thick. The fresh and heady scent of musky after-shave lotion came from the smooth jawline.

"Sorry, but I'm running a bit late." Rome apologized for not being ready. "I hope you don't mind waiting a few minutes. Make yourself comfortable." He gestured toward the array of chairs and sofas in the spacious living room. "There's liquor in the cabinet. Help yourself."

"Thank you," Lexie murmured, suddenly realizing she hadn't spoken until now.

With a faintly droll smile, Rome moved away, promising, "I won't be long."

Alone, Lexie began to focus her attention on the luxurious surroundings. She wandered into the living room, decorated in earth colors. It was tastefully simple yet bold, as aggressively masculine as its occupant. Lexie suspected it had been furnished by a woman, someone probably in love with him who had the talent to provide him with a background suitable to his image. A sultan's harem would have been more in keeping with his true character, she decided.

Moving to one of the sofas, she sat down to leaf through a business magazine lying on the coffee table. The political news Lexie knew and the rest she wasn't interested in. Finally she flipped it shut and glanced at her watch. How much longer would he be, she wondered. This constant waiting was wearing on her already frayed nerves.

Five minutes stretched into ten. Restlessly, her fingers worried the smooth turquoise stone in her necklace. In agitation, she rose from the table. She refused to pace and walked instead to the liquor cabinet where an ice bucket, glasses, and bottles sat.

The clink of a cube in a squat glass sounded loudly in the overwhelming silence of the room. Lexie splashed in a scant measure of gin and filled the glass with tonic water. Wrapping both hands around the fat glass, she turned and lifted it to her lips. Over the rim of the glass, she saw Rome walk in, stunning in an expertly tailored black suit that intensified his dark good looks.

"Ready?" she questioned, angered by the breathless

catch in her voice. There was no way of denying the physical effect he had on her, but Lexie had hoped to conceal it. Averting her face, she turned away to set her barely touched drink on a tray.

"Yes, but there's no rush, is there?" his low, well-modulated voice countered. "Since you haven't finished your drink, I'll join you."

"All right," Lexie smiled stiffly, not wanting him to see how anxious she was to leave and have this evening come to an end.

Her fingers closed tightly around the glass as he crossed the room to the liquor cabinet where she stood. With apparent calm, she watched him pour a shot of Scotch over ice cubes in a glass like her own.

The glittering dark eyes gave her a sideways look. "Waiting is hell, isn't it?"

"I beg your pardon?" She was startled by the unexpected content of his observation.

He turned to face her, the corners of his mouth deepening in amusement. "I'm referring to rushing around to arrive on time only to have your date make you cool your heels in the living room. It's a frustrating experience, isn't it?"

Nerve-racking, Lexie could have said, but she was suddenly hit by the discovery, "You deliberately made me wait for you," she said accusingly.

"For part of the time," he admitted without remorse. "I was legitimately detained by some phone calls just before you arrived. It seemed an excellent opportunity to show you how little a man likes to be kept waiting and how difficult it is to pretend he doesn't mind."

"That was a dirty trick!" she breathed angrily.

"Yes, it was," Rome agreed amicably, and sipped at the drink in his glass.

His assessing gaze skimmed Lexie from head to toe and back. It was not so much a stripping look as it was caressing. Her skin quivered in reaction to the pleasant but brief sensation.

"I'd forgotten how beautiful you are, Lexie," he commented.

"Flattery will get you nowhere, Mr. Lockwood." His compliment stiffened her.

"Rome," he corrected, and added, "it's going to be a long evening if our conversation is stilted with 'Mr. Lockwoods' and 'Miss Templetons.'"

He was right, but Lexie wasn't willing to admit that at the moment. She sipped absently at her drink and set it down. "I have dinner reservations for eight o'clock. It's seven-thirty now. Perhaps we should be going."

"Of course." He downed his drink and placed the empty glass near Lexie's.

Retrieving her handbag from the sofa cushion, she led the way to the door, waiting while Rome locked it behind them. Her car was parked at the curb and she walked half a step ahead of him toward it. He had to guess which it was; the economical little Mustang looked so out of place amidst all the other expensive models. But Lexie certainly wasn't going to make any apology for her mode of transportation.

"We did discuss role-reversal," Rome said when Lexie bent down to unlock the passenger side of the car, "but I think it would be less embarrassing for both of us if I opened my own doors."

"All right," Lexie was willing to concede that, but she added her own gibe, "I'm sure you can imagine how silly a woman feels sometimes when she has to wait in the car while the man comes around to open her door. It can be very awkward.''

"Touché," He smiled, and opened the passenger door while Lexie walked around the car to the driver's side.

What was awkward was driving with Rome Lockwood looking on. Lexie knew she was a competent driver—a very skilled one in fact—but she was self-conscious with him sitting beside her.

"I hope you don't have any prejudices against woman drivers," she commented, waiting for an opening in the traffic before turning the car into the street.

"None, only incompetent drivers," he answered.

Luckily Lexie didn't embarrass herself by grinding gears and the little car was on its best behavior, not stalling at stop lights or hiccuping across intersections. The traffic was fairly heavy and Lexie concentrated on her driving, thereby eliminating conversation. Still she was conscious of the dark gaze that strayed to her so often during the drive to the restaurant.

"I hope you approve of my choice," Lexie said when they arrived, not really caring whether he did or not.

"It's one of my haunts," said Rome as an attendant took the car to park it for Lexie. "Or did you check and find that out?"

"No. Frankly, it didn't occur to me." She returned his sideways glance with a sparkling look of battle.

The interior of the restaurant was almost intimidatingly elegant. A stiffly formal maître d'hotel stepped forward to greet them, smiling with pleasure, then his expression changing into a troubled frown.

"Mr. Lockwood, I'm terribly sorry, but I don't have

you on my reservation list. I'm sure if you can give me a few minutes I'll have a table for you," the man promised, almost profuse with his anxiety to serve.

"The reservation is in my name," Lexie inserted before Rome could respond, and the man drew back in surprise. "Templeton."

The maître d'hotel cast a questioning glance at Rome who was restraining a smile with difficulty. "That's correct, Charles. Miss Templeton has the reservation in her name."

As the man turned, Lexie saw him steal a glance at his reservation book lying open on a mock podium, to ensure that it was the truth. The look he gave her when he escorted them to a table plainly said that her action was a definite breach of etiquette. His attitude made Lexie's temper simmer.

A waiter was at their table almost the instant they sat down, filling the crystal goblets with ice water inquiring, "Would you care for a cocktail before ordering?"

Rashly Lexie asked, "Would you like one, Rome?"

"No, thank you," he refused, his gaze mocking her attempt to take charge in a man's world.

It only made her all the more stubborn. "We don't care for a cocktail," she informed the waiter. He darted a glance at a passive Rome Lockwood as he handed each of them a menu.

"The wine list, perhaps," The waiter suggested, offering it to Rome.

"The lady will choose," Rome replied, gesturing to Lexie, who gritted her teeth at his mockingly patronizing action.

She accepted the wine list from the stiffly disapproving waiter. Her knowledge of Rome Lockwood was sketchy, picked up in bits and pieces from what she had heard and seen. Too late Lexie remembered that he was considered something of a connoisseur of wines. She knew next to nothing about them.

"Is there a particular wine you would prefer?" Lexie tactfully attempted to conceal her ignorance.

It was as if those knowing dark eyes were aware that she was squirming inwardly, because Rome gave a mild shake of his head. "No. Whatever you choose I'm sure will be excellent."

Lexie wanted to scream in frustration. She guessed exactly what he was doing—letting her discover what it felt like when a woman deferred the choice to the man, especially if he was totally unfamiliar with her taste.

The wine list looked exceedingly formidable, with foreign brands listed that Lexie had never heard of. She only hoped that a restaurant such as this would not have bad wine on their list.

"A white wine," she murmured, narrowing the choice. "Something domestic, I think," Something she could read was what she meant, but she defended it by lamely joking, "To improve our foreign trade deficit." She gave her choice of a California Chablis to the waiter in what she hoped was a confident tone.

"A liter, miss?" he inquired. Neither the waiter nor Rome betrayed by expression whether her choice was a respectable one. Once it was given Lexie knew she couldn't retract it.

"Yes, please," she nodded.

The dinner menu, at least, was no obstacle to be overcome, but the prices made Lexie blanch. If she hadn't taken the money from her savings account, she would have been in a truly embarrassing position.

Since the choice of wine had been hers the waiter poured the sampling taste for her when he served it. Ill at ease, Lexie went through the motions of approving it. As far as she was concerned it tasted very good, but she was hardly an expert. The uncertainty must have been in her eyes when she watched Rome sip from his glass.

"Very good," he assured her.

But his approval only made her cross. "You know very well that I know next to nothing about good wine," she retorted.

"A good wine is one whose taste you like," he explained indulgently. "Do you like the taste of this one?"

"Yes." Her answer was curt and defensive.

"Then it's a good wine. There's no need to be defensive about your choice," Rome replied.

But she was, and it irritated her. Lexie had pictured herself making brilliant and witty conversation over dinner, but everything she said sounded stilted and forced. The meal was delicious, but for all the pleasure it gave Lexie, it could just as easily have been hash. By the time coffee was served she felt miserable while Rome seemed to be enjoying himself at her expense.

When the waiter brought the check on its miniature tray, he naturally started to set it in front of Rome, but was forestalled. "I'm the lady's guest tonight," Rome explained.

Lexie didn't know who was more embarrassed, she or the waiter, as he set the tray before her. She seethed at the wickedly laughing glint in the dark eyes watching her from across the table.

The waiter did try to ease the situation by joking with Rome. "You made a bet and the lady lost, huh?"

"You could say that," Rome agreed.

From her evening bag Lexie took out the amount of the check plus an adequate tip and placed it on the tray before returning it to the waiter. She flashed an angry look at Rome's bemused expression as the waiter departed from their table.

"Do you see how irritating it is?" she demanded.

"What?" he questioned with deliberate obtuseness.

"This stupid attitude you men have," Lexie muttered. "First the maître d'hotel with his shock that I'd made the reservations, then the waiter assuming that you would make the decisions and pay for the meal, then trying to find what he believed would be a plausible explanation when you didn't."

"It's been the custom for it to be a man's place to handle these matters," he reasoned.

"It's about time there were some changes, then," she retorted.

"Are you embarrassed at having to assert yourself?"

"No, I'm irritated," she retorted.

"The burning of a few bras can't change the habits of a lifetime, although I've noticed you haven't done away with yours." His gaze flicked downward to the rounded thrust of her breasts against the clinging fabric of her dress.

"And you're the type who would notice something like that," Lexie declared coldly.

"Would you prefer that a man not notice how attractive you are?"

"Not necessarily," Lexie admitted. "But I would like him to recognize that I have a mind and needs to be satisfied, the same as he does."

"Our acquaintance has been brief," said Rome,

"but I've noticed you have a mind. I have yet to find out about those needs you have to be satisfied."

"You don't have what it takes to satisfy them." She avoided the black infinity of his eyes as she slipped the shawl around her shoulders. "Shall we go?"

In answer, Rome uncoiled his long length from the chair.

CHAPTER FOUR

WHEN THEY ARRIVED at the nightclub Lexie had chosen to fill the rest of the evening, Rome gave her a sidelong look as they approached the entrance. "This is going to be an expensive evening. Are you certain you can afford it?"

"A woman would never ask that question of a man," Lexie smugly pointed out his lack of tact. "It would be a slur on his earning prowess."

"So instead of being considerate I've insulted you?" he remarked, his crooked smile acknowledging that she had scored a point.

"Precisely."

"My apologies." Rome inclined his head in a mocking bow of remorse.

Lexie couldn't help smiling in return, briefly allowing herself to be taken in by his charming ways, succumbing to the powerful force of his magnetism. Inside the club they found an empty table just as the featured singers took the stage.

Placing the money for their drinks on the table, Lexie acknowledged, but only to herself, that her cash had thinned more quickly than an overweight person on a starvation diet. Perhaps Rome had been right in questioning whether she could afford this lavish evening on the town. He probably had a fair idea what she earned. In a way she hoped he felt guilty that she was spending so much money.

Covertly studying his sculpted profile through the curling sweep of her lashes, Lexie didn't detect any sign of guilt as he watched the group performing. She realized he probably wouldn't feel guilty. His type rarely concerned themselves with matters other than those relating to themselves.

The entertainment negated the need for conversation. Nothing was demanded of Lexie, except to applaud at the conclusion of each song. She began to relax for the first time since the night's beginning. She didn't know whether to give the singing group credit or the wine at dinner followed by the present drink in front of her.

When the singing group left the stage for a break, Lexie commented, "They're very good."

"Yes, they are," Rome agreed.

"You've probably seen them perform hundreds of times, but this is the first time I've seen them," she said.

Rome swirled the drink around the ice cubes in his glass, watching it, an inwardly amused look to his expression. "Lexie, if I spent as many evenings out as you believe I do, how did I happen to have tonight free? A Friday night?"

His gaze caught and held hers. "I. . . ." Lexie faltered, "I was lucky, I guess." She recovered quickly.

"Or perhaps you chose a time so soon in hopes that I would have other plans and be forced to decline your challenge?"

"Before I made it, I found out whether or not you were busy tonight," she reminded him.

"So you did," he agreed. A dance combo had taken the place of the singers. As they struck up a slow ballad Rome glanced at the dimly lit dance floor, then back at Lexie. "Aren't you going to ask me to dance?" he mocked.

Denial was forming on her lips until the familiar phrase reminded her of how many times she had sat at a nightclub tapping her foot to some catchy song and making the same demand of her escort. No doubt it had happened to Rome. Now he was putting it to her. How could she refuse when she had set the rules for this evening?

But it was a grudging, "Shall we dance?" that Lexie offered.

Both rose simultaneously, but Lexie led the winding way through the clutter of tables to the small dance floor, lighted by an ever changing kaleidoscope of colored lights. In a relatively clear area of the floor Lexie turned. Rome stood in front of her, hesitating, a devil light dancing in his eyes.

"Do you want to lead or shall I?" he queried.

"You lead." Lexie managed a tight smile, simmering at the way he had taken every opportunity to taunt her with the impossibility of completely reversing their roles with ease. "I wouldn't want to be accused of stepping on your toes."

Rome laughed, a pleasant sound that shivered down her spine, making Lexie once again intensely conscious of his considerable attraction. When he took her hand and slid his arms around her waist, Lexie felt an electric current shoot through her. It added a new tension to her finely strung nerves. She knew she was unnaturally stiff in his arms but she didn't want to risk coming in closer contact with him for a moment.

"Relax." His low voice spoke in the vicinity of her ear. "Enjoy the music."

If he had asked her to enjoy anything else, Lexie would have ignored him, but that was an inducement she could submit to as she let the languorous beat of the music carry her away. She allowed herself to be drawn closer until she felt the brush of her jaw and chin against her hair. The music swirled about her, evoking its own romantic spell.

One arm was on his shoulder, her hand resting near the back of his neck. The other arm, Rome folded to hold still against the black lapel of his jacket. A sensation of intimacy flowed through Lexie and she arched away from his chest, tipping her head back to warily search his face.

There was a musing curiosity about the look he gave her, oddly warm and gentle. "I always thought redheads had green eyes, yet yours are a vivid blue," he commented absently.

But Lexie didn't want compliments from him, knowing they came too easily to his lips. "Like limpid pools?" she mocked.

"I hope I would have been more original than that." His lazy smile ignored her stinging retort.

"I'm sure you would," she agreed, but hardly in praise.

"Are you Irish?"

"On my father's side," Lexie admitted.

"Me, too, but on my mother's side."

"Black Irish, of course." Her gaze touched on the raven darkness of his hair and eyes.

"Of course."

"Rome darling!" A female voice declared in sheer delight. "I didn't know you were here tonight. Where are you sitting? You must join us."

Half of the words were said before Lexie could turn her head to see the chic blonde dancing near them with a disgruntled-looking partner. The man was plainly unhappy to see Rome. He was attractive in a bland unassuming sort of way and Lexie knew it would be no contest for him to be matched with the likes of Rome Lockwood.

"Hello, Stella—Andy," Rome greeted both of them, but responded to none of the woman's questions.

The pressure of the hand at the back of Lexie's waist would have guided them away from the couple but the song ended, making it impossible.

"You can't have been here very long" Stella declared, "or I would have noticed you. Or maybe you've been hiding in some dark, out-of-the-way corner?"

Cold gray eyes were turned on Lexie, jealousy radiating from the petitely fragile blonde inspecting her and not liking what she saw. Lexie felt her monetary worth being assessed, the hard gaze stripping her silver dress for the status of an appropriate designer label. She wasn't bothered that the blonde couldn't find one.

"We arrived in time to catch the show," Rome admitted.

"I just can't keep up with you!" The girl laughed, a brittle sound. "Another new girl! You must introduce us, darling."

His sideways glance took note of Lexie's veiled amusement before Rome complied with the request. "Lexie Templeton. Stella Van Wyck and Andy Crenshaw."

"Templeton?" The blonde's partner frowned in surprise at the name. "From the newspaper?" he added in disbelief.

"The same," Lexie admitted, realizing he had made the connection.

Stella was not nearly as quick, only the prompting word "newspaper" provided the clue. "From the newspaper?" she repeated, and darted a wide-eyed look at Rome. "You don't mean she's the one who's been saying all those vicious things about you."

"The one and only," Lexie stated before Rome could confirm it.

"And you're here? Tonight? With her?" Stella looked at Rome as if he had taken leave of his senses.

"Why not?" The arm that had been resting lightly at the back of Lexie's waist increased its pressure as Rome glanced to her, a mocking glint in his eyes reserved strictly for her, it seemed. "I've met the enemy and she's mine."

"Hardly," Lexie denied the claim in a cool dry voice, and heard his low throaty chuckle.

"I've heard of some unorthodox methods used to attract your attention, Rome, but Miss Templeton—" Stella's glance at Lexie was contemptuous "—has certainly gone to extremes. She was successful obviously, since she got what she wanted and is here with you tonight."

The color drained from Lexie's face at the completely false accusation that had been leveled at her. She felt the silent speculation of Rome's gaze. Before she could voice any denial the band began playing another song and the four of them had to either dance or make room for others crowding onto the floor.

"Excuse us." Rome's arm was pushing her away from the dance floor.

They were halfway back to their table before Lexie attempted an indignant correction. "I didn't do any of this to attract your attention, Mr. Lockwood. If I wanted to chase a man my approach would be much more straightforward."

"I'd like to see that—your straightforward approach," Rome added to clarify his meaning.

At the table Lexie turned to confront him. "You don't believe me," she accused. "You think I said all those things and asked you out because I wanted you. Your overinflated ego probably thinks every woman is just dying to be with you. Well I'm not! You don't interest me at all."

"I believe you." But his look was one of total amusement, eyes glinting in laughter at her angry denunciation.

"Then you won't object if we leave." She was still furious, but his acceptance frustrated further discussion of the matter. "It's time this evening was brought to an end."

For Lexie, the drive to his apartment was accomplished in smoldering silence, but Rome seemed carelessly relaxed despite the cramped quarters of her car. There was a parking space at the front curb and Lexie whipped the easily maneuverable small car into it.

Both hands on the wheel, the engine running, Lexie turned to him. "Here you are, delivered safe and sound."

Rome didn't move, his arm draped negligently along the back of the seat. "Aren't you going to walk me to the door?"

With savagely controlled movements, she switched off the engine and pushed open her door, stalking around the car to meet him as he climbed out of the passenger side. Lexie didn't trust herself to say a word until they reached his apartment door.

"I've seen you to your door," she declared tightly. "Is that good enough?"

"Thank you." He nodded with mock politeness. "I would invite you in for coffee or a drink but it's only our first date and I wouldn't want you to get the impression that I'm easy." The corners of his mouth were twitching at the effort of keeping a straight face.

Lexie drew in a breath and held it, angered at the way he was constantly voicing all the trite things women had ever said, flinging them in her face with such curious delight. All that was lacking from this scene was a giggle.

"Good night!" she snapped, and started to pivot away.

"Wait a minute." Rome caught at her arm. "You're forgetting something."

"What now?" Lexie demanded in exasperation.

An arrogant brow arched to mock her. "The goodnight kiss."

"Oh, God!" It came out in the angry exhalation of a breath. "Do you honestly think for one minute that I'm going to kiss you—that I want to kiss you! This whole evening has been a fiasco—a farce! With you laughing all the way. Well this is one laugh you aren't going to have!"

"I quite understand." Rome let go of her arm with a mild shrug of his shoulders.

"Good. I'm glad!" Lexie flashed.

"It's a difficult thing to carry out with any aplomb," he continued. "The romantic climax of any date seems to be the kiss at the door. There's always so much emphasis on it; so much is expected to happen with it."

Mentally her mouth was dropping open. Rome was doing it to her again, reeling her in like a fish on a hook, the barbs sinking in so she couldn't wiggle off. All she could do was squirm.

"Kissing is taken for granted." He watched her knowing and enjoying her discomfort. "But timing is so essential—when to make the move. And there's the problem of not bumping noses or heads. Should the pressure be gentle and sweet, or passionate, sweeping the person off her feet? I quite understand why you wouldn't want to attempt such a difficult task." The faint emphasis on the pronoun was really referring to her sex. "Men don't have any choice, not if they want to take the girl out again. A good-night kiss is compulsory for a man."

Rigid with anger Lexie knew she was well and truly caught. She glared at his handsome, mocking face for an instant then succumbed to his blackmail. It wasn't easy to take the initiative, especially when he wasn't offering any assistance. First of all, she didn't know where to put her hands. Finally she rested them on his wide shoulders for balance as she rose on tiptoe.

Her breath caught when her lips touched his firmly molded mouth. Its warmth and pliancy was a revelation as she kissed him, aware of his hands moving to her waist. Lexie wasn't indifferent, and cautious wisdom drew her away.

"Not bad," Rome murmured. "Let me show you how it's done."

Before she could voice her refusal the hands at her waist were pulling her back, arching her against him while his descending mouth took possession of hers. Worldly and experienced, Rome demonstrated his mastery of the art. A warm wonderful confusion was totally enveloping Lexie, leaving her defenseless.

Her hands were spread over his shoulders, fingers half-raised in a paralysis of surprise and bewilderment at her reaction. Her mouth was mobile beneath his, allowing his pressure to part her lips. Rome deepened the kiss with sensual brilliance, exposing her senses to raw new emotions that hungered for something more.

She was shaky inside when he ended the kiss. The sweep of her lashes veiled the look in her eyes, but the breath she had been holding was released in a revealing sigh. Despite all that she moved firmly away from him, recognizing now that she was not quite as immune to his virile charm as she had believed.

"Good night," she said and thanked heaven that her voice was steady.

"This is the point where you're supposed to make arrangements for another date," Rome said.

"No way." Lexie shook her auburn head vigorously.

The combination of his mocking voice and the absence of his touch broke the spell of enchantment she had been under. She could look at him now with all her formal abhorrence for his type.

"I don't care to see you again," she said emphatically. "We've both carried out this experiment unwillingly and I certainly don't want a repeat performance. Neither, I'm sure, do you."

"Still," Rome paused, a half-smile crooking his

mouth, "thank you for a most...enlightening evening."

"For that, you're entirely welcome," Lexie returned. "Good night."

"Good night, Lexie." He finally wished her the words that brought the evening to a close.

But it wasn't quite as easy to close her mind to the memory of any of it. During the drive to her own apartment Lexie considered herself every kind of a fool for finding physical gratification in his kiss. It was an empty promise that gave no hope of fulfillment—not for lack of potency, but for lack of endurance.

One thing it had shown her—under the right circumstances, men like Rome Lockwood could be irresistible. She, who knew better, had reacted like a colorful moth drawn to a flame, a black flame. Her wings had been singed, but she was still capable of flying away, thank goodness. Tonight was one night she was going to block out of her memory.

It would have been easy to do. She had the desire and the willpower to forget Rome Lockwood, but pressure was exerted by outside influences to recall him and their date. On Saturday morning Ginger plied her with questions demanding to know everything that happened.

"The evening was a total mockery." Lexie sat at the small breakfast table. Dressed in her rumpled robe, she wished the cup of coffee could erase the bad taste left in her mouth from the previous night's fiasco. "Rome Lockwood found it all very amusing. As for me—I just ended up poorer than before."

"It couldn't have been as terrible as you say," Ginger insisted. "Didn't he kiss you or anything?"

"Yes, he kissed me." The instant the admission was out, Lexie glanced sharply at the beaming face of her roommate. "Don't look at me like that," she snapped. "It was just a kiss, nothing special."

"Oh, come on now," Ginger murmured skeptically, determined to find a happy ending.

"You are as taken in by his Don Juan image as he is," Lexie retorted. "One kiss is not going to change my opinion of him. And I'm certainly not going to fall in love with him. I know what kind of merry hell he would lead me through. I've seen it before, and it's not going to happen to me."

"You've seen it before? When? With whom?" Ginger asked curiously.

"It doesn't matter." Lexie clammed up and took a sip of her coffee.

"Did he ask you out again?"

She set her coffee cup on the table with an abruptly impatient move. "What does it take to convince you that we were both *trapped* into going together last night," Lexie demanded. "Rome Lockwood was just as glad to see the back side of me as I was to walk away. If we never see each other again, it will be too soon."

"You don't have to bite my head off. I just asked a simple question," Ginger protested with a trace of indignation.

"All right." Lexie struggled to hold her temper. "To answer your simple question—no, Rome Lockwood did not ask me out again. Do you mind terribly if we change the subject?"

"No," Ginger agreed reluctantly, finally accepting the fact that Lexie had not been on a "dream" date the night before.

Lexie had barely convinced Ginger when the telephone rang. It was Shari Sullivan, and Lexie had to answer almost the same questions all over again, and parry them with the same noncommittal replies.

On Sunday morning Ginger was quick to waken Lexie and show her the newspaper, specifically Shari's column. As Shari had said, Lexie and Rome were her headlines. Lexie wasn't surprised by that, but the photograph that accompanied the column did surprise her.

It took an instant for her to realize that it was a contrived photograph. From the newspaper files, someone in the photography department had taken a picture of Rome and one of Lexie, and fitted them together to make it appear that the newspaper photo was one of them together.

When she went to work on Monday, it was just as bad. Everyone wanted to know about her date with Rome Lockwood; every detail from what they wore to what they had eaten or drunk. Their obsession with his name became exasperating.

Stepping into the elevator, Lexie punched the numbered button for her floor and waited for the doors to close. She'd had her Wednesday lunch at a little delicatessen some distance from the newspaper office. She had chosen it because there she wouldn't have to endure the endless comments about Rome Lockwood from her co-workers.

"Going up? Wait!" A familiar voice called. The elevator doors closed on a hand that was thrust between them. Soundlessly the slid open to permit Gary Dunbar inside. "Hi," he said, smiling self-consciously at the sight of Lexie.

"Hi, yourself," she returned.

"Just coming back from lunch?" At her affirmative nod, he said, "Me, too. Where did you eat? I didn't see you at the restaurant next door."

"I grabbed a sandwich at a deli," Lexie explained. Minus any further obstruction, the elevator doors closed.

"Are you doing anything Saturday night?" Before Lexie could answer, Gary rushed on. "I'm doing an article on a neighborhood drama club. They're... uh...giving a performance Saturday night, and I've got a couple of free tickets. I wondered if you'd like to come along."

"Sounds like fun," she agreed, since it was infinitely preferable to spending the evening alone.

"I don't know how much fun it will be," he said with a disparaging shrug. "It's just one of those amateur things. I can't offer you the lavishly produced entertainment that Rome Lockwood probably could."

"I'm not interested in his brand of entertainment. And if I hear his name once more, I swear I'll scream." Lexie issued the threat tautly, certain she would never be able to escape the mention of his name.

"I didn't mean to upset you—" Gary began an immediate apology.

"Let's make a deal. I'll go out with you Saturday night on the condition that his name never enters the conversation," she said.

"Agreed," Gary smiled and looked somewhat relieved.

It wasn't as easy to persuade the others to drop the subject.

The Saturday-night date with Gary was like a breath

of fresh air. She was able to relax and enjoy herself knowing that she wouldn't have to defend herself against a lot of curious questions the following morning.

As in all things the interest gradually died out. After two weeks her life had begun to return to normal. Even Shari had stopped being so resentful at Lexie's lack of newsworthy details about the date.

Lexie paused at the doorway of the columnists' office alcove. "You wouldn't by any chance have a cup of coffee to spare for me?" she asked, glancing at the steaming cups both Shari and Ginger were holding.

"Of course." Shari turned her swivel chair around to fill a Styrofoam cup with coffee from the glass pot on the hot plate behind her.

Lexie accepted it gratefully and flopped wearily into a straight-backed chair. "What a morning!" she groaned, and nearly scalded her tongue when she tried to sip the hot coffee.

"Hectic, huh?" Shari offered sympathetically.

"You can say that again," sighed Lexie.

"I was just asking Shari what she thought I could buy Madge for her wedding shower. What did you get her?" Ginger asked.

"An electric blanket. I found one on sale last week." Lexie blew into the cup trying to cool the hot coffee. "This seems to be the year for weddings. Are there any single girls left in this building?"

"Three of them in this room," Shari replied.

"I suppose I could always buy her some sheets or towels." Ginger was mulling over the shower gift. "I simply have to buy something on my lunch hour today. It's going to be too late when I get off work and the shower is at seven."

"Tonight?" Lexie sat up in her chair.

"Yes, tonight," Ginger nodded.

"I can't make it," Lexie declared with a resigned sigh. "You'll have to take my gift, Ginger, and apologize to Madge."

"Why can't you go?"

"Mike's just informed me that Mac and I have to cover that fund-raising dinner tonight. The Senator is flying in from Washington to attend and a couple of other politically important VIPs will be there," she explained.

"You mean you have to work tonight?" Ginger questioned in protest.

"Surely you've learned by now, Ginger," Shari inserted, "a reporter doesn't have an eight-to-five job, but works any and all hours."

"With a salary commensurate with that of the slave she is," Lexie added, "because a reporter is compensated by the glamor of his job." Lexie joked about her profession, but she had entered it knowing it wasn't one of the high-paid careers unless the reporter gained a national name.

"I'm learning fast," Ginger grimaced, going along with them. "But it's a shame you're going to miss the shower tonight. It'll be fun."

"You've been putting in a lot of extra hours lately," Shari observed. "Your vacation is coming up, though, isn't it?"

"Next month," Lexie replied without enthusiasm.

"And you're off to London," the other girl said, smiling.

"Not this year." Lexie flashed a quelling look to Ginger not to reveal the reason.

"Why not?" Shari frowned. "That's all you've been talking about for the last six months."

"I've decided I can't really afford it," she shrugged. "The last thing I want to do is fly over there on a shoestring. I'm going to see London in style when I go."

"What will you do on your vacation?" asked Shari.

"Sleep." Lexie laughed away her answer.

"Seriously," Shari protested. "You aren't going to stay around here, are you?"

"I imagine so." Lexie took a drink of her coffee, cooled now. "I don't have anywhere else to go."

"Yes, you do," Ginger inserted. "In that postcard you got from your father last week, he asked you to come out and visit him." Then her light complexion colored furiously. "I wasn't really reading your mail, Lexie," she apologized. "It's just that, well, a postcard is so open."

"It's okay." Lexie wasn't offended.

"Your father lives in California doesn't he?" Shari frowned as she tried to recall.

"Palm Springs," Lexie admitted.

"There's your solution. Spend your vacation in sunny California," Shari offered. "You can stay with your father and it won't be all that expensive."

"No, thanks." Lexie finished her coffee and rose. "Dad and I don't get along unless there's the width of a continent between us. The less we see of each other, the more we like each other. You know the old saying—familiarity breeds contempt. That's us."

"It seems a shame for you to spend your vacation sitting around your apartment," Shari persisted.

"That's the way it goes sometimes." Lexie turned to

her roommate. "I probably won't have a chance to see you again before tonight, so don't forget to take my gift with you tonight to Madge's shower. It's wrapped and everything, inside my closet.

"I won't forget," Ginger promised. "Have fun."

"Ha!" was Lexie's scornful response.

In Lexie's experience these fund-raising dinners always seemed like a three-ring circus with something going on somewhere all the time. She often wished for another pair of eyes and ears, or possibly three or four sets.

The dinner that evening in the huge banqueting hall proved no exception. For Lexie there was more involved than just listening to the speeches and making notes. There was always behind-the-scene maneuvering going on and it was prudent to pay attention to who was sitting with whom.

Mac, the photographer who had drawn the assignment with her, was proving to be a distraction. When he wasn't darting around getting a picture of this person or that one, light meters and lenses dangling around his neck, he was sitting beside her at the press table munching on a cold hamburger and French fries. His on-the-run meal was becoming singularly unappetizing to Lexie with each passing minute he left it beside her.

"Can't you wait until this is over to eat?" she whispered in protest.

"I'm starved," Mac hissed. "I haven't eaten since yesterday noon, and that was a cold hot dog."

Lexie shrugged expressively and tried to concentrate on the current speech. The paper bag rattled as Mac dived into it for more fries.

"What happened to last night's meal?" she questioned keeping her voice down, trying to not distract the others. "And this morning's breakfast?"

"I was up all night covering that fire. I slept through breakfast and caught hell from Mike for coming in late. Then I missed lunch." He listed his woes. "It's for sure I'm not going to sit here while all these fat cats stuff themselves on steak and I'm fainting with hunger."

After receiving that justifying explanation Lexie forced herself to ignore his munching. As she listened to the speaker, her gaze swept over the tables. It hadn't occurred to her that all the moneyed people in the area would have received invitations to the political fund-raising dinner, including Rome Lockwood.

She realized it when she saw him sitting at one of the tables. She hadn't noticed him there before and wondered if he had just arrived. To her knowledge he had never actively campaigned for anyone, although his support had often been courted, as it was now. One of the campaign chairmen for this year's election was leaning over talking to Rome in hushed tones.

Had he noticed she was there? Was he aware she might have been assigned to cover the dinner, Lexie wondered, and immediately banished such questions from her mind. What did she care? Rome Lockwood was nothing to her and vice versa.

Her gaze strayed often to his table after that. Strictly in the course of reporting, Lexie rationalized. If Rome did decide to back a particular candidate, that would be news, her purpose for being there. If Rome ever glanced her way, it wasn't when she was looking at him.

It was just as well, she convinced herself. She wasn't interested in having Rome acknowledge her presence—she had had enough of that. There was one good thing about his attendance at the dinner—she had forgotten about Mac's noisy meal in the interim. Now it was concluded with only the paper remains stained with ketchup and mustard to remind her.

CHAPTER FIVE

WHEN THE DINNER and speechmaking were finished people began mingling and the atmosphere became informal. Mac, who had a facility for remembering faces, was snapping shots of the noteworthy persons in attendance. Lexie had cornered one of the mayor's aides and was pinning him down about the mayor's stand on a current tax issue.

There had been a time when she was first starting out that it had been difficult to get people to talk seriously to her, although being so strikingly attractive, she had never been overlooked. Even now there were times when her questions were answered with indulgence instead of being taken seriously. But more and more people were beginning to respect the reputation she was building for herself. The mayor's aide was quite anxious that she understand the mayor's position.

He had her undivided attention until she happened to catch a glimpse of Rome Lockwood over the man's shoulder. Rome was talking to two men whom Lexie recognized as being politically active in the state. She also noticed that Stella Van Wyck was with him, and a second woman, a brunette, also seemed a part of the group.

Unfortunately, as far as Lexie was concerned, Stella chose that moment to glance in her direction. She felt the blonde's gaze narrow on her. Then with a melodic laugh that carried to Lexie's ears, Stella turned back to Rome, catching at his arm and nodding toward Lexie.

"Look, darling," she said, "there's that smart red-headed reporter you were with the other night. Is she here to check up on you?"

Rome turned, a white smile flashing across his tanned features. Despite the distance between them Lexie felt the magnetic power of his charm as his dark gaze caught her look and held it. Then he said something to the others, something her hearing couldn't catch. The others laughed, all eyes focusing on her.

Her cheeks burned as she quickly tore her gaze from his. It required all her strength to center her attention on the man standing before her, talking earnestly.

"It's a confusing issue," he was saying, "with points on both sides. But the mayor feels his stand is the best for the community as a whole. You do understand?"

Lexie glanced at her notes. They were sheer gibberish. She hadn't heard a single word the man had said, except for the last few sentences. She had missed it all. How could she lose her concentration like that, simply because Rome Lockwood looked at her?

"Yes, of course, I understand," she lied. "Thank you for explaining it."

"My pleasure, Lexie." He used her Christian name but for the life of her she couldn't remember his.

"Excuse me." Smiling, she moved away, her steps taking her in the opposite direction to both the aide and Rome Lockwood.

Her throat felt dry. She slipped her notepad and pen into her shoulder bag and headed toward the massive coffee urn sitting on one of the long tables. She poured herself a cup of coffee and turned. Rome was standing in front of her.

"Hello, Lexie," he said quietly, a warm pleasant smile lifting the corners of his mouth.

"Goodbye." She pivoted at a right angle to walk away from him.

"Hey!" Rome laughed. "Not so fast. I came over here to talk to you."

Blue fire flamed in her eyes. "Don't you think I've provided enough laughs for you and your friends?"

He tipped his head to the side, indulgently curious. "Did you think we were laughing at you a minute ago?"

"Weren't you?" she countered.

The overhead lights made his hair seem darker than ebony. "No," said Rome, "but I can see you aren't going to believe that."

"I'm not."

"I've been thinking about you." There was a quiet intimate quality to the low-toned remark.

"I'm not impressed," Lexie rejected the message. "Why don't you go back to Stella?"

"Jealous?" Rome mocked, impish lights dancing in his dark eyes.

"Of course not!" she snapped.

"Good, because if it was Stella I was interested in I'd be over there talking to her now. Since I'm here, it should be obvious that it's you I'm interested in."

"And I told you last time I saw you that I wasn't interested in you. I thought I'd made that plain," she retorted.

"That's what you told me," he conceded, "but your kiss said something different."

Lexie averted her head. "I wouldn't put too much stock in a kiss, Mr. Lockwood. A girl has to kiss a lot of toads before she finds the prince."

Rome chuckled. "You enjoy trying to put me down, don't you?"

"Yes."

"Why? Are you envious? Is that what made you become a feminist?"

"What?" She glared at him, angered by his implication.

"However unfair it may be, it's true that if a single girl leads the kind of life that some bachelors do she would sacrifice her good name. It's the old double standard that you resent so much."

With that teasing gleam in his eye Lexie couldn't tell whether he actually believed what he was saying or if he was saying it just to bait her. Before she could make up her mind, Lexie's temper snapped at the lure.

"Do you honestly think that I would want to be a...a—" for a reporter, she had an extraordinary amount of difficulty finding the appropriate word "—a philanderer like you?" Lexie winced inwardly at her choice. Its meaning was accurate but it was hopelessly outmoded.

It drew a smile as she had known it would. "Lexie Templeton, a philanderer," repeated Rome. "That's a provocative thought, isn't it?"

"Go away!" Lexie cried softly in a burst of impatience.

"Hey, Lexie, there you are!" Mac came up on her unexpectedly. "I've been looking all over for you."

"I stopped for a cup of coffee," she defended her presence away from the mainstream of activity.

"Listen, I gotta cut. I have all the pictures Mikes's gonna need," he said, lifting his camera as if she could see them in the black box. "If I'm late getting home again tonight the old lady's going to have my hide. I know I promised to give you a ride, but you can find somebody else to take you home, can't you? Or catch a cab maybe? Mike will be good for the fare."

Lexie opened her mouth to say she was ready to leave now, but Rome stepped forward, "I'll see that Lexie gets home."

Mac wasn't even surprised to see Rome with her—not after all the gossip that had gone through the office. "Swell, Mr. Lockwood!" he declared with relief, and started moving away. "See you tomorrow, Lex!"

He was gone, trotting off toward the exit door. Lexie would have had to run to catch up with him. She glanced angrily at Rome. Why did he have to butt in?

"Whenever you're ready to leave, let me know," he said. "I'll be somewhere around."

She started to tell him that she wasn't interested in having him take her home, but immediately she thought better of arguing.

"Thanks," Lexie said instead, and was rewarded by the glimmer of surprise in his look. "There's a couple of other people I want to interview before I leave, so it will be awhile yet. I'll find you when I'm ready."

"All right." Rome moved away.

Lexie finished her coffee, waiting until she saw where Rome had stopped, then she began mingling with the various reporters and dignitaries on the opposite side of the room. She picked up pertinent bits and pieces from various sources but when her opportunity came to slip out a side door, she took off.

She hurried down the deserted hallway toward the main entrance of the building. There were always plenty of cabs in this vicinity; with luck, she would find one waiting outside. As the large doors came into view, she saw Rome standing beside them. Her steps slowed at the knowing light in his dark eyes.

"Ready?" he asked when she reached him.

"Yes." Not for anything would Lexie admit that she had been trying to slip away from him.

"My car is just outside." He reached for the door, holding it open for her.

Thwarted in her attempt to escape, she took pains to conceal her frustration as she accompanied Rome to his car. Inside the luxury sedan she gave him her address and relaxed against the cushioned seat upholstered in a rich gold velour. Maybe if she ignored him.... The thought formed hopefully.

"I expected more of an argument," Rome commented as the car purred into the traffic.

"About what?" Lexie deliberately pretended ignorance at his meaning.

"About letting me drive you home." His sidelong look said she knew very well what he meant.

"Why should I?" She ran a caressing hand over the velvety-textured seat cushion. "Talk about the lap of luxury, I'm riding in it." She laughed with a trace of sardonicism.

"You mean a person like myself does have his uses?" taunted Rome.

"On occasions." Lexie gazed out through the windshield, pretending an indifference to him that she was far from feeling. "I was surprised to see you at the dinner tonight. I didn't think you attended such functions as a rule."

"As a rule, I don't," he admitted.

"Why did you tonight? Are you planning to become involved in politics? Offer your support to one of the candidates or the Party?" she questioned, feeling safe behind the shield of a reporter.

"No, my family has made it a practice not to be actively involved in the political mechanics of government," Rome answered.

"Then why were you there?" Lexie repeated her first question.

"I know you'll find this hard to believe, considering how frivolous you think I am, but I'm interested in finding out about the men who might be representing me in government, local, state or federal."

"You were just being a public-spirited citizen, is that it?"

"See?" He swung a lazy glance to her. "I told you you'd find it hard to believe, coming from someone like me. Is that why you accepted the ride? To discover my motives?"

Lexie shrugged and stared out of the side window. "Your name is always news. If Rome Lockwood is behind a particular candidate it's even bigger news." If that was what he wanted to believe, that suited her.

"Will you have dinner with me on Saturday night?"

Her first startled reaction was "What?" followed immediately by "No."

"Why not?" Rome spared a glance from the traffic, his manner calm and expectant.

"Because I don't like you. I've told you that before," Lexie answered flatly. "You're only interested in me because I haven't fallen at your feet like every other female you've come across. It's a case of wanting the unattainable, the beckoning of green grass. It's your ego surfacing again, wanting every woman to adore you. Sorry, but that's not me. We're two different people."

"You're probably right," he conceded unexpectedly. "We would make an unlikely pair, a feminist and a philanderer."

"I'm glad you see it." Lexie was horrified by the disappointment she felt that Rome had not pursued her acceptance of his invitation.

"By, the way, what happened to your car?" he said, switching the subject with disgusting ease. "Or did you arrange to ride with the photographer to economize?"

"My car is in the shop being repaired, I hope," Lexie tried to follow the change just as fluidly. "It refused to start tonight and I had to call Mac to pick me up for the dinner."

"Is it anything major?"

"I hope not. I couldn't afford a big repair bill." That slipped out before Lexie could stop it, her mind immediately flitting to the expensive evening with Rome. "The mechanic didn't think so," she qualified.

"What are you doing for a car in the meantime?"

"I can ride back and forth with Ginger, my roommate. She works for the paper, too." Lexie was determined to make light of the problem.

"What about your assignments?"

"Until I get my car back I'll simply have to hope Mike will send a photographer along and I'll be able to go in his car. If not, I can probably persuade him to stretch my expenses to a cab fare."

"You're welcome to use one of my cars," Rome offered.

"No, thank you. I'll manage," Lexie refused.

"Sure?"

"I'm sure," she nodded. "My father taught me never to owe anybody favors."

"In case you don't want to pay what they want to collect?"

"That's the idea," she admitted.

"So you're afraid that if you accept the loan of my car you might not like the favor I would ask from you in return?" He was laughing at her, however silently.

"Do you blame me?" countered Lexie. "Considering your reputation?"

"Oh, no." This time Rome chuckled aloud. "After all, I'm a dastardly fellow."

"Stop it!" She was suddenly impatient with the way he was constantly making fun of her wariness.

"Seriously," he tried again, controlling the amusement in his voice, "if you find yourself in need of transportation, don't be afraid to accept my offer. You can borrow my car with no strings attached, I promise."

"It wouldn't make any difference," she protested. "I would still feel obligated."

"We may never be lovers, Lexie, but I'd like to think we could be friends," Rome argued gently. "They say opposites attract. Who could be more opposite than you and I?"

"Lovers," "attract"—they were heady words, the kind that disrupted Lexie's pulse. The car turned a street corner onto the block where her apartment building stood and she was saved from having to make a response.

"It's the second building on the right," she directed him. "You can park in front." When he had stopped the car, she shifted the strap of her shoulder bag a little higher and reached for the door handle. "Thanks for the ride," she offered as she pushed the door open and stepped quickly out.

Before she could swing the door shut Rome was turning off the engine and sliding out from behind the wheel. Their gazes locked across the top of the car.

"It isn't necessary," Lexie started to protest.

"No self-respecting man would let a girl walk to the door alone," he reminded her, the grooves deepening around his mouth.

With a sigh of resignation she turned away from the car. Rome's long strides soon brought him beside her. Lexie was supremely conscious of the last date and the parting kiss. Even now the imprint of his mouth was on her lips and she couldn't shake away the memory. Damn his attraction! And damn her susceptibility to it!

In the narrow and dimly lit hallway outside the door, she was aware of her breath coming quickly. She rummaged frantically through her bag for the key, trying not to show how desperate she was. Rome would wait there until she had it in her hand, an inner sense told her that. At last she came up with the key ring, but Rome took it from her and inserted the key in the lock, turned it.

He didn't open the door nor did he move out of her

way. A dangerous feeling of intimacy raced through her, yet there was nothing seductive or threatening in Rome's manner. It was just his innate charm having its effect on her.

"Are you going to invite me in for coffee?" He held the keys in his had, his gaze teasing.

"No," it came out abruptly. "It's late and my roommate is probably asleep."

"It wouldn't be a good idea anyway, would it?" It seemed more of a statement than a question, accompanied by an easygoing smile.

"No." Lexie agreed, and held out her hand. "My keys."

"You won't reconsider about dinner on Saturday?" Rome continued to retain possession of her key ring.

"No." She didn't trust herself to say more than that.

Her legs were beginning to feel shaky. He was much too close, overpowering her with his sensual attraction. He offered her the keys and she took them, but before she could draw her hand away his had closed around it.

"It's my turn to make the move," he said.

Her mind protested but her body had a will of its own, pliantly allowing her to be drawn into his embrace, her head tipping back to receive his kiss. Her arms wound around his neck, as she was caught in the enchantment of his warm mouth.

Surrender quivered through her limbs, igniting a thousand fires whose heat seemed to melt her bones. His mouth hardened in its claim on hers, seeking and demanding in its utter ravishment. Lexie knew she should have felt shame or disgust at her abandon, but there was only the heady glory of his kiss.

Weightless in his arms, she had a curious floating

sensation, yet his lean muscular body was real. So were the strong hands that forced her softer shape to fit the hard contours of his male form. The pressure of his mouth was exquisitely demanding, taking, seeking and finding. His caresses aroused and inflamed her, a hand sliding up to her arm to draw it tighter around his neck. Her fingers curled into the sensual thickness of his black hair.

The deafening roar of her heartbeat echoed wildly sweet through her veins; flesh pulsed in the pagan tempo. On its downward glide from her arm, his hand hesitated on her rib cage, then lightly curved itself to the swell of her breast. Lexie trembled at the intimacy, inflamed by it. She didn't want to react this way, to respond this way, but a stronger, more primeval instinct was directing her.

Rome seemed driven by it, too, but he was stronger than she. Or maybe it was a part of the dark spell he cast on her; Lexie only knew she was helpless against the soul-destroying fire of his embrace. Tears moistened her lashes. It was so beautiful, and so wrong.

When Rome released her lips to press his mouth to her cheek, his breath was as ragged and disturbed as her own. Her lips throbbed with the passion he had made them feel and give. Her heart seemed lodged in her throat and she could not even gulp it down.

"You're a witch," Rome accused, and returned to take a mouthful of her parted lips offered in sacrifice. "A fiery enchantress."

No, it was the other way around, her mind insisted. He was the enchanter, but she could say nothing as he took short, punishing tastes of her lips.

"Have dinner with me on Saturday," he commanded. Lexie felt the flexing of his muscles, his male power being branded forever onto her flesh. "At my place." His hand completed its encirclement of her breast, cupping its ripeness. "I'll cook the meal if that will satisfy your feminist heart."

She was powerless to deny him anything. "Yes." And she was certain in that instant that she was insane.

"Seven o'clock on Saturday. You'll be there," ordered Rome.

"Yes."

He pulled her arms from around his neck, letting her hands rest lightly on his chest. His dark gaze blazed possessively over her face and Lexie marveled at the way eyes that were so dark could seem so incredibly bright.

Cupping her cheek with his hand, Rome traced the porcelain-smooth line of her jaw with his thumb. Then he let it seek the curves of her soft lips, outlining them. His thumb forced them apart to feel the white edge of her teeth. Her tongue touched its tip. With a stifled groan, Rome slid his thumb under her chin and let his mouth take its former place.

Lexie was driven backward to the wall of the hallway by the unchecked force of his kiss. The lower half of her body was pinned there, crushed by the thrusting weight of steel-hard thighs and hips. With a bent arm braced against the wall for support, Rome arched her to him. Every nerve end was aware of his demanding male need and the hollow ache in her stomach longed for fulfillment.

His mouth blazed a fiery path to her neck and the lobe of her ear. The moist warmth of his breath blowing unevenly against her skin sent shivers of passionate ecstasy racing down her spine. Lexie clung to his jacket, overwhelmed by emotions too powerful to deny.

"Invite me in, Lexie." There was a husky, disturbed quality in his voice.

"I...can't." It hurt to say it when she should have been relieved. "The landlady...she lives downstairs. She doesn't allow us to have...male visitors. Besides, there's my roommate," she finished, wishing she had simply refused instead of explaining.

She heard the deep, self-controlling breath Rome took as he lifted his head, relieving the pressure that held her to the wall. His mouth crooked as he gazed at her, a rueful smile that held a trace of frustration.

"Then you'd better go in," he told her, "before I make love to you in the damned hall."

Despite the amusement lacing his tone, it was no joke and Lexie was well aware of the fact. It was difficult to move, even after Rome had levered himself away from her. Weak and shaken, she managed to reach the door, trembling under the touch of his gaze.

"Lexie." She turned at the quiet sound of her name, the knob already turned, the door ajar. His hand lightly caressed her cheek, a fingertip trailing across her lips. "Dream of me?" Rome asked.

In the blink of an eye, it seemed, his hand was withdrawn and he was striding down the hallway. Dazed and confused by what she considered to be a betrayal of her self-respect, Lexie entered the apartment.

As she locked the door she remembered that she had agreed to see him again, to have dinner at his apartment. How could she be such a fool? The misty fog of raw passion began to dissipate under the cold breeze of reality. Senses previously controlled by desire surrendered to the control of her mind.

From somewhere in the darkened apartment Lexie heard the sound of muffled sobs. It was obviously Ginger. More than anything, Lexie wanted to steal into her room and solve the problem of her own wretched agony, but she couldn't ignore the plaintive sounds of her roommate. She didn't bother with a light but made her way by instinct to the other tiny bedroom.

"Ginger?" She paused in the doorway, hearing gasping attempts to hold back the sobs. "Are you all right?"

"Yes," was the sniffing answer.

As much as she wanted to, Lexie couldn't accept that. "Do you want to tell me what's happened?"

There was more sniffling and the creaking of the bed springs as Ginger sat up. "Yes, but don't. . .don't turn on the light, please."

There wasn't any need to. The street light outside shone through the window illuminating the tear-stained face and the rumpled golden hair Ginger was pushing away from her face.

Lexie walked to the bed and sat on the edge, feeling suddenly like a very old lady coming to console a frightened child. Only there was a little child inside herself that was frightened, too. Who would console her?

"What's wrong?" Lexie pushed aside her own needs. "Did something happen at the shower tonight?"

"No, it's Bob," Ginger choked out the answer, her voice constricted with pain.

"I might have known," Lexie murmured. Wasn't it always a man?

"We. . . we had a fight," her roommate hiccuped out the explanation, scrubbing the tears from her eyes with shaking fingers.

"What about?" Lexie prompted.

"He wanted me to go out with him tonight but I told him I couldn't because I had to go to Madge's shower. Bob thought I could just go over there and drop the presents off and. . . and go out with him. When I wouldn't do that, he got mad. He said if a. . . if a bunch of girls meant more to me than he did, then maybe we should call it quits." Tears began streaming down her cheeks again. "When I got home from the shower I called him but he didn't answer. I've called and called and called, but he isn't there. Oh, Lexie, he really meant it." Her shoulders began shaking in silent sobs. "He's out with somebody else—I just know it!"

"And it's probably a good thing, too. I know that sounds cruel," Lexie apologized, "but do you really want a guy who expects you to give up your friends for him?"

"You don't understand," Ginger wailed. "I love him!"

"He doesn't deserve it," Lexie argued. "He doesn't appreciate you. You're just wasting your love on him, and he doesn't want it. All he wants is—"

"No!" Ginger's strident cry wouldn't let Lexie complete the sentence. "You never did like Bob. I don't know why I ever thought you would understand. Just go away and leave me alone!"

With a sigh Lexie rose from the bed and left Ginger alone with her misery. Ginger was right; she hadn't trusted Bob. And who was she to give advice when she didn't practice the wisdom that she preached?

A pain shot through her heart. "Dream of me," Rome had said. That was going to be easy to do. His touch, his kiss, his image haunted her. Yes, she would dream of him, Lexie realized, but it would be a dream that would soon turn into a nightmare of hurt and anguish.

Fool that she was, didn't she know it? Or didn't she care? Hadn't she learned anything? Or was it all inevitable?

CHAPTER SIX

LEXIE KNEW SHE COULDN'T keep the dinner invitation. She didn't dare. At her desk the next morning, she thumbed through the pages of the telephone directory for Rome's number. After a fruitless search, she dialed information. The operator informed her that his telephone number was unlisted.

Back to the thick telephone book. She began leafing through the pages for his office number. She had to give him her decision and offer brisk apologies, even though she knew he wouldn't like it. He might argue with her, but she was determined not to give in to his persuasions. Her fingers had just located the telephone number for Lockwood Enterprises and she was reaching for a pencil to jot it down when a shadow fell across her desk and the pages of the telephone book. Lexie glanced up and blanched guiltily under the shrewdly curious eyes of the female columnist.

"Am I interrupting something?" Shari Sullivan inquired in a too-smooth voice.

Lexie quickly closed the phone book. "No, nothing." Her voice was thin in its rush to assure. "I was just going to call the garage to see if my car was fixed yet."

"You took your car into Sam's, didn't you?" the columnist remembered. "You won't find him under the L's, but you might find Rome Lockwood's number in that section.''

"How clever of you to notice,'' Lexie remarked, and smiled a tight, false smile.

"What happened? Did you leave your notebook in his car last night?'' Shari asked in a voice reminiscent of a cat's purr.

"Last night?'' Lexie repeated. Then she demanded, "How did you know about that?''

"Oh, I have my own private grapevine,'' came the throaty reply, filled with deliberate mystery.

"Only one person knows about last night, besides myself and Rome. Mac told you, I suppose,'' Lexie guessed with grim accuracy. "I sometimes think that man never knows when to keep his mouth shut.''

"Was it a secret, honey?'' The bleached blonde's eyes widened with false innocence.

"Of course it wasn't a secret,'' she answered impatiently, not wanting to put too much importance on the incident since it would only increase Shari's interest. Shari might be a friend, but as a reporter, Lexie didn't trust her to keep anything quiet. "But I can just imagine the way Mac made it sound when he mentioned it to you.''

"Lexie, honey, please don't try to convince me that Rome Lockwood gave a lowly little reporter a ride home simply out of the goodness of his heart.'' There was something cunning in the smile she gave Lexie. "Knowing his reputation, I'll never believe chivalry had anything to do with his motive. So what gives?''

"Nothing.'' Lexie stubbornly tried to make light of the incident. "Rome happened to be talking to me when Mac said he had to leave and asked if I could hitch a ride home with someone else. Maybe courtesy dictated that Rome should offer me a lift. I don't know and I don't care."

"How many times have you seen him these last couple of weeks?" Shari changed her tactics, switching from sly innuendo to direct questions.

"I haven't seen him at all." Lexie could truthfully and vigorously answer Shari's prying question.

"Haven't you?" A finely drawn eyebrow was delicately arched to dispute Lexie's statement. "I suppose it was purely coincidence that Rome was attending that political function last night."

"I told you before that I'd seen him at similar things occasionally," Lexie reminded her.

"So you did," Shari admitted. "But the two of you could just as easily have arranged to meet there. Your car was conveniently in the garage, and Mac is notorious for his disappearing acts once his part of an assignment is finished."

"Your two and two are adding up to five," Lexie declared.

"You can't blame me for being suspicious. It all looks very arranged." The columnist put suggestive emphasis on the last word.

"Well, it wasn't. It was purely accidental." Considering the disastrous results of the meeting—disastrous at least as far as she was concerned—accidental seemed the appropriate word.

"When will you be seeing him again?" Shari wanted to know, watching her closely.

Lexie tried to cool the warmth in her cheeks. "I don't know," she replied, knowing that there was still the dinner engagement to be cancelled. "Probably the next time Rome hobnobs with the politicians."

"Do you mean that he hasn't asked you out?" The question was asked as if the blonde already knew better—which was impossible.

"If he did, Shari, I wouldn't tell you," Lexie retorted. "As a matter of fact, I would hope you'd be the last to know. You've ferreted out all the information from me that you're going to get."

"Is that any way to talk to a friend?" The older woman looked offended.

"If you *are* my friend, you'll let the subject of Rome Lockwood drop and not use me to claw your way to the top," Lexie challenged.

A coldness swept over the columnist's face. "We're both in the business of news, Lexie."

"Then go find your news someplace else instead of rehashing old gossip." A sigh of irritation took much of the steam out of Lexie's reply.

After Shari had walked stiffly away, she opened the phone book again and found Rome's office number. His secretary informed her that he wasn't in. Lexie tried several times the next two days to contact him at his office during business hours, but he was always out when she called. Lexie couldn't help wondering if it was deliberate. But she never left a message nor asked that he return her call, nor even identified herself. She didn't want her name joining a monumental list of other female callers.

All her suspicions that he was avoiding her had to be thrown out. On Friday, Rome called her at the newspaper. She held the receiver in her hand, too stunned by the voice on the other end of the line to speak.

"Lexie, are you there?" His questioning voice held a hint of amusement.

It prodded her into answering. "Yes, I am. Sorry. I'm glad you called, I. . . ."

"It suddenly occurred to me that you might need transport tomorrow night," Rome interrupted to explain why he called. "Is your car out of the shop yet?"

"Yes. I. . . ."

"Templeton!" Mike barked behind her. "How come you're still here? I thought I told you to get over to city hall."

"Just a second." She cupped her hand over the mouthpiece of the receiver, and glanced impatiently at Mike, "I'll be leaving in a second," she promised.

"See that you do," he warned, but despite his gruffness, he wasn't really angry.

Lexie removed her hand, "Sorry," she said to Rome, "I. . . ."

"You're busy. I'll see you tomorrow night at seven, my place."

"No! Wait!" Lexie protested, "No, I. . .can't make it." The last part of the sentence trailed off lamely as a dial tone buzzed in her ear.

"All right, let's get going Templeton!" Mike urged behind her.

Lexie stared at the telephone in frustration, then, grabbing her shoulder bag and note pad, headed for the exit. She knew she had missed her one and only chance to tell Rome her decision.

By Saturday night, Lexie was being pulled in two directions at the same time. One insisted that she simply ignore the invitation she had accepted and not show up at Rome's apartment. The second wanted her to go, tell him she couldn't stay and leave.

As she was dressing, she kept searching for a third choice and found none. The door to the apartment opened and closed, and a few seconds later Ginger called to her.

"Lexie, I'm home. Where are you?" The rattle of paper bags indicated that her roommate's shopping expedition had been successful.

"In the bedroom." The taut state of her nerves made Lexie's voice sound shrill. She ran a smoothing hand over the flame-colored curls of her hair before turning away from the mirror to walk to the doorway to the living room.

Ginger's back was to the door as Lexie entered. "I didn't realize it was so late. I hope you haven't eaten dinner. I picked up some Chinese food on the way back and got a bit carried away. There's plenty here, more than I can eat."

"I'm not really hungry." Lexie's nervous stomach began to roll at the thought of food.

Ginger turned, a protest forming on her face until she caught sight of Lexie. "Are you going somewhere?" she frowned. "I don't remember you mentioning that you had a date tonight."

"I don't." Lexie hadn't confided to her roommate about her meeting with Rome or the invitation to dinner she had foolishly accepted. There was too much risk that Ginger would let it slip to Shari Sullivan. And then, too, Lexie had been less than understanding when Ginger had been all confused about Bob.

"What are you all dressed up for?" her roommate persisted.

"I'm...just going out for a little while," she said evasively. "When is Bob coming over?"

"Eight. That's why I grabbed all this Chinese food, so I wouldn't have to fix anything to eat here," Ginger explained. "Do you want me to put some of it in the refrigerator so you can have it when you come back? You might be hungry by then."

"Maybe," Lexie replied, conceding the possibility. Once this meeting with Rome was over, her nerves might settle down. "Thanks."

"Where are you going? Shopping?" Ginger started toward the kitchen.

"No place special. Just out for a while," she lied.

Ginger stopped and flipped her long corn-silk hair over a shoulder. She stared curiously at Lexie, a puzzled frown knitting her forehead.

"Are you sure you don't have a date?" she questioned again.

"I told you I'm just going out for a while," Lexie repeated, but avoided the girl's look.

"You *are* going on a date," Ginger accused in breathless rush. "I'll bet it's with Rome Lockwood, isn't it?"

"Whatever gave you that idea?" She tried to laugh it away, but ended up sounding guilty.

"Shari said the other day that she was positive there was something going on between the two of you. I didn't believe her, but it's true."

"No, it isn't," denied Lexie.

"You never said a word to me." The full force of her spaniel eyes was directed at Lexie. "You wouldn't have told me if I hadn't guessed you were going to meet him."

"Look, I don't have a date with him," Lexie insisted, then fell back on the truth. "Actually I do have a date with him, but I'm breaking it. I'm supposed to have dinner with him tonight. Unfortunately he has an unlisted telephone number so I couldn't call him to cancel it. As much as I'd like to, I just can't stand him up. So I'm going over to his place to tell him the dinner is off."

"That's why you didn't want any of the Chinese food I bought—because you're going to have dinner with him. Why didn't you say so?" Ginger asked in a confused voice.

"I'm not going to have dinner with him," Lexie repeated. "I'm not eating with you because I'm too nervous."

"Nervous? Why?"

"Because I know he's going to argue with me, that's why." And he could be so persuasive, she thought. But she didn't tell Ginger that, not after all the preaching she had done. "And don't you dare breathe a word of this to Shari. I had all the comments I could stand from everybody in the building the last time I went out with Rome. It's finally been forgotten, and I don't want Shari churning things up again by printing something in her column."

"If you feel that way, then why did you say you'd go with him tonight?" It didn't make any sense to Ginger.

"I think I was out of my mind at the time," Lexie admitted. "Promise me on your mother's life that you won't tell Shari."

"I won't. You can trust me, Lexie," her roommate promised.

Lexie glanced at her watch. The hands pointed to a

few minutes past six-thirty. "I'd better leave. Unless I get caught in traffic, I should be back before Bob comes."

"Good luck."

By the time she had driven to Rome's apartment her toes were like ice cubes. She paused in front of Rome's door. Before she could retreat she pushed the doorbell. This time there was no waiting, no time to think. The door opened and Rome was there, so casually male, so devastatingly handsome; a satyr with his dark, knowing eyes and that black mane of hair.

His attraction grabbed her throat, robbing her of the words she had come to say. She could only stare, her heart beating faster. The lightning touch of his gaze licked over her shape, setting fire to her skin through the white of her slacks and the flame-orange blouse of gauzy fabric.

"You're right on time." As he reached for her hand, it fluttered quite naturally into his and Lexie was drawn into the apartment not against her will because she had no will.

Once inside Rome brought her effortlesly into the circle of his arm. There was a mesmeric quality to his gaze as a tanned hand cupped the side of her face, fingers tangling in the flame gold of her hair.

"I thought you might not come," he murmured. A mixture of delight and triumph was in his soft laugh. "Does it give you any satisfaction to know how uncertain I am of you, Lexie?"

"None." Was that her voice, so clear and calm? His gaze dwelt on her lips a warning instant before his mouth moved toward them. Miraculously she turned her head a fraction and he found only the corners of her mouth. "I shouldn't have come," she said.

"Don't...." The word came out sharply, fingers tightened with painful pressure along her face. Just as suddenly, Rome relaxed, laughing and changing his demeanor from that of a demanding lover. "Don't you trust my cooking?" he mocked.

"It isn't that." Lexie moved out of his arms and he didn't attempt to stop her. She pretended to brush the hair away from her cheek but she was really trying to erase the tingling of her skin where he had touched her. "I didn't plan on coming here tonight. I tried to get hold of you to tell you that, but you have an unlisted number and you weren't in your office when I phoned. When you called me yesterday you hung up before I could tell you that I'd changed my mind and wouldn't be here."

"Why did you come then?" Rome eyed her steadily.

"I don't like people who break appointments without warning," she defended herself. "I think it's inconsiderate and horribly rude, so I couldn't just not show up."

"I see." Rome turned and walked across the room to the liquor cabinet. "You agreed to come the other night."

"The other night was a mistake." His back was to her and she found it was easier to talk without his dark gaze levelled at her. "I don't want to become involved with you."

There was the rattle of ice cubes and the splashing of liquid. When Rome turned, he held two glasses in his hand. He crossed the room and handed one to Lexie, who accepted it rather absently.

"You feel it would mean sacrificing your principles," he said.

"I know it would." Lexie stared at her drink. Gin and tonic—he had remembered.

"I had the impression the other night that you wanted me to make love to you."

"Look—" she bit at her lower lip in agitation "—I'm not going to try to deny that I find you very attractive sexually, but I neither like you nor respect you as a person, and I believe those are two essential ingredients in forming an intimate relationship."

There was a resigned yet arrogant arch to his brow. "That says it all." Rome lifted his glass and took a quick swallow. He gave her a piercing look. "Now that you've told me, I suppose you intend to leave without sampling my culinary efforts."

"I can't stay now—you must see that," Lexie insisted.

His mouth twisted wryly. "All I know is that I have two expensive steaks marinating in the kitchen—an entire meal prepared for two that you expect me to eat alone."

"I can't help that."

"Yes, you can. There's no need for all that food to go to waste. Since you are here," he reasoned, "you might as well stay for dinner."

"I . . . ." Lexie hesitated, uncertain, torn by what she wanted and what was wise.

"I promise I won't force myself on you," Rome said with a grin, and lifted his glass in a toast. "We'll just be two friends sharing dinner."

She was twenty-four; she was supposed to be an adult. What was she going to do? Run from his apartment like a frightened teenager?

"Two friends," she agreed, and touched the rim of her glass to his.

She had been truthful when she said she didn't trust him—any more than she trusted herself in his company. As she lifted the glass to her lips she studied him over the rim, looking for any sign that his suggestion masked an ulterior motive, but there seemed to be none.

"Bring your drink out to the kitchen," said Rome. "You can watch me put the steaks on and fix the salad, unless you would prefer to sit around the living room and wait."

"No, I'll come with you." She had had her share of waiting.

To get to the kitchen, they had to go through the dining room. It was a small informal room, which Lexie had seen in decorating magazines described as a breakfast room. Obviously Rome didn't do any entertaining in his home on a large scale.

An intimate table for two was beautifully set with an ivory linen tablecloth, crystal and sterling silver. Two silver candle holders flanked a bowl of fresh fruit. The succulent cluster of grapes reminded Lexie of something out of a Greek orgy scene. She could easily visualize Rome plucking a grape and carrying it to her lips; her stomach curled at the sensuous thought.

The kitchen was efficiently small, with every modern convenience imaginable. Rome moved familiarly around it, setting the steaks in a pan and into the oven. Lexie stood uncertainly in front of the refrigerator and had to step away when Rome walked to it.

"All you have to do is supervise," he told her. "I'll do all the work."

"That will be a change," was the falsely bright response Lexie offered.

He began placing a variety of ingredients on the counter. The bacon was in the refrigerator; he took two strips and put them in a skillet. While it was frying, he added sugar, water, oil, vinegar, ketchup and an assortment of spices to a container. As he turned the sizzling bacon in the skillet, he darted a glance sideways at Lexie. "How do you like the picture of a man slaving over a hot stove?"

"I like it." She smiled faintly.

"You would."

"Is there anything I can do?" It wasn't easy standing around watching him. The freedom of looking at him was too unnerving.

"No." Then Rome reconsidered. "You could take the candles off the table, since the evening no longer requires a romantic setting."

"I'll do that." Lexie turned to the dining room, then stopped. "Where do you want me to put them?"

"On the sideboard along the wall is all right."

Lexie experienced a twinge of regret as she removed the candles from the table, which was silly. She didn't want to share a candlelight dinner with Rome Lockwood. The bowl of fruit remained as the sole centerpiece, the pale green grapes contrasting with the red ripeness of apples—the fruit of temptation—and the burgundy and yellow skin of the peach.

When Lexie returned to the kitchen, Rome was adding chopped eggs and crumbled bacon to the dressing and expertly tossing it all together with fresh spinach leaves in a bowl. Never once did he seem uncertain about the next step.

"You are a good cook, aren't you?" she commented.

"Mm," he agreed without false modesty, tossing away the half compliment. "My parents taught me to be self-sufficient. Can you cook?"

"Adequately," Lexie responded to the teasing question. "But you'll certainly never have to marry in order to have a woman around to do your cooking."

"A wife has other uses."

"Such as bearing your sons," she said dryly.

Rome clicked his tongue in reproof. "Your chauvinism is showing. What about daughters?"

"My comment was what a man would say," Lexie replied, defending her answer.

"Of course," he agreed mockingly.

"Do you do your own laundry, too?" She switched the subject.

"Why? Are you going to offer to do it for me?" Rome eyed her wickedly.

"No, I hate doing laundry. I was going to see if you'd do mine," retorted Lexie.

"Bring it over anytime." He picked up the salad bowl, missing the flush that colored Lexie's cheeks. "You're in for a treat tonight, fresh spinach salad with dressing à la Rome, my speciality," he said.

"It looks good," she admitted.

"It is. A few minutes in the refrigerator to let it all chill together and you'll be begging for my recipe when you taste it," he mocked. With the salad in the refrigerator, Rome turned to the grill. "How do you like your steak?"

"Rare to medium rare."

When they finally sat down to the table, Lexie

couldn't find fault with either the meal or the company. The food was delicious. She wasn't sure she could have done as well. The conversation didn't drag painfully as it had that first time, but Rome was directing it. Lexie responded naturally to his easy wit and general subject matter.

Halfway through the meal, Rome offered, "More wine?"

"Please." She raised her glass for him to fill. "Do you have any idea how embarrassed I was trying to choose from that wine list, knowing I was sitting across the table from a man with a reputation of being a connoisseur?"

"I have a fair idea," he admitted, the grooves around his mouth deepening. "Your eyes can be very expressive at times. I remember they were a very electric blue, shooting sparks when you looked across the table at me."

"You weren't any help," Lexie retaliated. "You wouldn't give me a hint."

"I know." Rome filled her glass, then his own. "The restaurant's wine list was impeccable. It was impossible for you to make a bad choice."

"That's what I was hoping," she said, smiling.

By the time the meal was finished, the bottle of wine was empty. Lexie was sipping the last of it, enveloped in a rosy afterglow of good food, good wine and good company.

"That was delicious," she sighed and lifted her glass in a salute to Rome. "My compliments to the chef."

"They are most welcomely received." He returned her salute with mocking formality, inclining his dark head in acceptance. With their glasses drained, he said, "We'll have coffee in the living room."

Lexie was almost too comfortable to move. Reluctantly she pushed her chair away from the table and agreed, "Okay, but first I'll help you with the dishes." She started gathering them to carry to the kitchen.

"No," Rome refused. "We'll take them to the kitchen and stack them on the counter. I may cook, but I draw the line at standing in front of a sinkful of dirty dishes. The maid can wash them when she comes."

Together they carried the plates, glasses and silverware into the kitchen while Lexie teased, "Then that's why you'd marry—to have a woman to wash your dishes?"

"That's a good reason, isn't it?" Rome pretended to be serious, but there was the twinkling light of laughter in his eyes. "Here." He handed her a tray with a coffee service on it. "You can take this into the living room."

Entering the living room, Lexie set the coffee service on the low table in front of a long sofa. She sat near one end and poured coffee from the pot into two china cups. When Rome appeared seconds later, Lexie continued her task without glancing up.

"Cream or sugar?" she asked.

"Neither." He walked to the sofa where she sat. "My kitchen talents don't stretch to rich desserts, so I decided we would end the meal on a continental note with cheese and fruit. Is that all right?"

Lexie stared at the bowl of fruit he set on the table, a touch of panic momentarily blinding her to the plate of cheeses and crackers. Her thoughts returned to her previous erotic fantasies with uncomfortable swiftness. Rome joined her on the sofa, but with a friendly space between them.

She swallowed and answered in what she hoped

would be her previously carefree tone, "That's fine." But she reached for the cheese. "After that meal, I don't need the calories of a rich dessert."

His gaze raked her length, his look indicating he found nothing wrong with her fully curved slimness, but he made no reference to it when he spoke. "If you're counting calories, maybe you should have some fruit. Would you like a peach?"

He took one from the bowl as relief swept through Lexie that he hadn't said "grape." "Sounds good," she admitted.

Instead of handing it to her, Rome took a knife and completely circled the peach in a lengthwise cut. He split it open and lifted out the pit with the knife point, then handed the two halves to Lexie.

"Thank you." She set one half down and took a bite of the other.

Juice squirted from the ripe, pulpy flesh. Lexie swallowed and laughed self-consciously as it trickled down her chin. She quickly wiped it away with her fingertips and started to lick the excessive moisture from her lips, aware of Rome's narrowing gaze on her.

"No," he said.

Her heart thumped against her ribs as he leaned forward and kissed the juice from her lips with sensual drugging sweetness. The breath left her lungs. Her senses were swimming when he raised his head.

"You shouldn't have done that," she protested weakly, looking down and away from his face so he couldn't see how deeply affected she was by his kiss.

"Sorry—" he didn't sound it "—but your lips looked so delectable I couldn't resist them." He moved back to his previous distance. "Cigarette?" he offered in an offhand way that suggested they had just been discussing the weather instead of kissing.

"No," she refused, unable to make the transition as effortlessly as he did.

"Do you mind if I smoke?"

"Not at all." The rest of the peach remained on the table. Lexie couldn't risk a repeat of what had just happened.

Smoke swirled in a puffy cloud. "I never have asked where you're from," Rome commented.

"Originally from Massachusetts—Salem, but like most families, we moved around a lot when I was growing up," she answered.

"From Salem? I knew you were a witch." He laughed, then asked, "What brought you back?" He sounded interested, mildly curious. "Did you attend college here?"

"No, I graduated from U.S.C., Southern California, but I always wanted to come back east and work. So when I graduated, that's just what I did."

"How do you like your job as a reporter?"

"I'm not doing it for the money, that's certain, so it must be because I like it."

"Where's your family now?" Rome asked.

Yes, Lexie thought, *let's talk about my family.* It was just the subject she needed to get a grip on herself. Or maybe it was all that wine. Maybe she needed to sober up. She picked up the saucer and cup, balancing them on her lap.

"My mother died when I was eight. I don't have any brothers and sisters," Lexie answered his question. "There's only my father and me. He lives in California."

"You must have been close," Rome commented. "I can't imagine that your father likes you living so far away."

"Dad realizes that every little girl has to grow up and leave the nest," Lexie shrugged, not bothering to deny his first remark, but there was a wry twist to her lips.

"Daughters do that, don't they?" He smiled and sipped his coffee. "I didn't ask if you'd like some brandy in your coffee. Would you?"

"No." She was almost convinced the wine had been too much.

His cigarette smoked in the ashtray as he rose from the sofa. "I think I will." He crossed the room to the liquor cabinet and added a dash of brandy to his cup. Before returning he paused beside a built-in stereo system. "Do you like music?"

Lexie was about to say she did when there was a click and the music of a string orchestra drifted through the room. Suddenly it was all too much—the wine, the music, the intimate atmosphere. She set her cup down and rose.

"It's time I was leaving," she announced decisively.

Rome stopped, looking at her with a raised brow. "So soon?"

"Yes," Lexie insisted. He set his cup down and walked over to stop her. "Thank you for dinner. I enjoyed it very much." How trite she sounded!

"Are you busy tomorrow?" he asked.

"Yes," she lied. She would have the whole day to herself. Bob was back on speaking terms with Ginger again and her roommate had been starry-eyed all day with her glorious plans for the weekend with Bob.

"Doing what?" Rome pursued.

"Things." Like doing the laundry, cleaning the apartment, trying not to be bored.

"Why are you running out, Lexie?" The piercing question sliced away her pretense of normality.

"I'm not running. I'm walking," she insisted, unwilling to admit she felt the need to escape from him.

"Why? Do you think the time has come for the seduction scene?" he asked in an arid tone.

"Hasn't it?" Lexie retorted. "You've wined and dined me. Now there's dreamy background music. When are you going to turn the lights down low?"

"And what if I don't try to seduce you?" His gaze had sharpened to a dark intensity, difficult to hold and impossible to break away from. "What will you do? Will you think I'm waiting to lull you into a false sense of security before I make my move? It would never occur to you that I might want you to stay because I want your company?"

"Oh, please, don't start that friendship argument again," she cried, her exasperation tinged with sarcasm. "It isn't friendship you want from me."

There was something ruthless in the set of his jaw. "It seems to be a case of damned if I do and damned if I don't. What have I got to lose?"

Her backward step was never completed as he caught at her arms and pulled her to him until she was brought up to the muscular columns of his legs and the solid wall of his chest.

"Rome, don't!" Lexie tried not to give way to virginal panic, making her protest firm and faintly threatening.

"You're like fire and ice to me—" his hand slid into her hair roughly, yet a caress; a steel band circled her to make her a prisoner of his embrace, "—with your flame-red hair and ice-blue eyes. One minute you're burning me with your beautiful fire and the next, you're freezing me out. I've been cold all night. It's time you warmed me."

Lexie turned her head and eluded his mouth but Rome wasn't deterred. He kissed her eyes, nose and cheek, found that particularly sensitive spot below her ear and nibbed at her lobe. Her legs grew weak under his sensual assault, tremors quivered through her at the raining storm of his kisses.

Blood pounded in her ears like the roar of thunder, primitive and awesome. In the end it was she who sought the fulfillment of his kiss, turning her head and stopping the ravishing exploration of his mouth with her lips, but Rome parted her lips with practiced ease.

As destroying as the previous kisses had been, Lexie realized they had been a match flame compared to the blazing raging fire consuming her now. Rome seemed to know just how to keep the fire burning out of control.

When he swept her into his arms and carried her back to the sofa, Lexie's arms curled around his neck with artless abandon. Her senses ruled supreme. She was aware of the feel of his rippling muscles like a heady aphrodisiac, and the intoxicating taste of his warm mouth with its lingering traces of brandy and wine.

Seated on his lap, Lexie felt the roaming caress of his hands adding more fuel to the fires of her passion. His searing mouth followed the jutting curve of her chin to the hollow of her throat while his fingers dispensed

with the buttons of her blouse with an ease that should
have alarmed her.

When the gauzy material was pushed aside his hands
spanned the bareness of her waist, lifting and arching
her up to give his lips free access to the swelling curve
of her breasts and the tantalizing valley between them.
Lexie gasped at the raw sexuality of his intimate touch
and slid her fingers into the black mane of his hair.

Then Rome was forcing her backward onto the sofa
cushion, his weight pinning her to them as he followed
her down. She was molded to his length as his mouth
returned to the ready surrender of her lips. Their body
heat fused them together. Lexie knew only that she
wanted to touch every inch of him, to find that promised mindless glory of total knowledge.

CHAPTER SEVEN

SHE COULD FEEL THE HAMMERING of his heartbeat, the disturbed deepness of his breathing. There was satisfaction in knowing she had aroused him as fully as he had aroused her. It gave her a sense of power, however uncertain of her ability to wield it. The hot moistness of his breath touched her cheek as his mouth moved to the vulnerable point along the cord of her neck.

"One of us is crazy," Rome muttered near her ear.

The sound of his voice broke the paralyzing hold on her throat. Her flesh might have surrendered totally to his will, but her mind still controlled her voice. And her mind still knew how hopeless it was to love him.

"It's me," she cried softly. "I don't want to do this."

"Yes, you do," Rome insisted. "You've wanted it as much as I have from the minute you walked in the door."

"That's not true," she denied.

"It is." He kissed the corner of her mouth and she turned her head to one side, straining away from his kiss.

"No," she repeated her denial, adding, "I didn't even want to come here tonight."

"Yes, you did, or you wouldn't be here." Rome kissed the corner of her eye and the wing of her brow, not deterred by her soft denials or the sudden elusiveness of her lips.

"That isn't true," she protested. "I tried. . . ."

"Stop pretending." He cut her short. With elbows for support, Rome lifted his head and cradled her face in his hand, forcing her to look at him. "If you really didn't want to come tonight, all you had to do was write me a note and drop it in the mail or leave it in my office or slip it under my door, telling me you'd changed your mind. The only reason you wanted to reach me by phone was that you wanted me to talk you into coming."

"No!" breathed Lexie.

"Yes." The black fire of his gaze smoldered over her face. "You're here because it's where you want to be. You want to be talked into staying. You want me to make love to you as much as I want to make love to you. Admit it, Lexie."

"No." She had to swallow back the sob that rose in her throat. "I don't!"

Abruptly Rome pushed away from her, rising from the sofa and taking a step away, all in one liquid movement that left her suddenly very cold and alone. Startled, shattered by his statement, Lexie was slower to move, rising shakily, trying to shake off the stinging truth of his claim.

She stared at his handsome, aggressively male profile. A distant part of her mind registered the fact that the gray silk of his shirt was unbuttoned, exposing the bronze of his naked chest and the raw animal virility it conveyed. But her thoughts were focused on trying to explain somehow.

He was aloof and withdrawn, seemingly miles away.

She rose, her hand reached out to touch his arm and draw him back. The instant her fingers came in contact with the hard muscles, her touch became a gliding caress.

"Rome, I . . . ." She began.

Violently he flung her hand away from him.

"Stay away from me unless you've decided it's rape you want now!"

Lexie flinched from the lashing flick of his angry voice and stood motionless in the paralyzing grip of her agony. She knew she deserved that. Rome was fighting to control all the passion she had aroused in him.

"Sorry, I . . . ." He clamped his mouth shut on the rest of the sentence as if suddenly deciding he had no cause to apologize.

Lifting a hand, he raked it through the thickness of his hair, rumpling it more than Lexie's fingers had. He crossed the room to the liquor cabinet, putting distance between them, and splashed a healthy measure of brandy into his glass.

"I'll leave," Lexie said quietly.

There was no more point in staying. Rome had made her face the truth. She couldn't pretend any more that if she stayed, it was for any other reason than to be in his arms and to know his possession. The second truth was that she could never face herself again if she did.

"No!" Rome's strident denial brought her up short. "Not—yet," he added in a much more controlled tone, but was still a savage bite to it. He tossed down a swallow of brandy. "We need to talk yet."

There was a brooding quality about his handsome features that gave him a darkly dangerous look. It surprised Lexie. She had expected Rome to use his considerable charm as he had in the past, or react with the thwarted anger of a spoiled child denied something he wanted. Certainly she hadn't anticipated this display of inner anger, this grimness. It confused her because it seemed so out of character.

"There isn't anything left to say, Rome," she replied. "It's all been said."

"No, it hasn't. And for God's sake, button your blouse!" he snapped harshly. "Or are you the type that likes to torment and tease?"

Crimsoning under the downward slide of his gaze that touched so derisively on the exposed swell of her breasts, Lexie hurriedly pulled the front of her blouse together and began fastening the buttons.

"Look, I'm not going to pretend that I didn't want...." What was the use in stating the obvious? She sliced the rest of the sentence away and went straight to the point. "I'm not cut out to be a one-night stand—to be just another passing fancy."

"Is that all you think you are?" he demanded.

"Isn't it true?" Tears sprang to her eyes and she had to blink them back. "Maybe you want me for your lover, your mistress, but once the newness wore off I'd be just another pretty face in a long line of pretty faces."

"How can someone as young and beautiful and intelligent as you have so little confidence in your ability to make a man love you?" The muscles along his jaw flexed, revealing the tautness of his control.

"There's always going to be someone who's younger, prettier and smarter," Lexie retorted. "And I'm going to grow old, wrinkled and dumb."

"So will I."

"No," she disagreed. "Men like you acquire character lines and experience and more women chasing after you."

The tears in her eyes were welling up to the point where she couldn't see. Any minute she was going to start crying, and that would be the final humiliation. She had already made a big enough fool of herself. With a quick turn she walked swiftly to the door.

"Lexie!" Rome impatiently called her back but she didn't listen.

Before she could turn the doorknob his hand was there holding the door shut. Summoning all her pride she turned her liquid blue eyes to him.

"Let me go, Rome," she requested. "If you take me in your arms, I'll probably beg you to make love to me. But if you have an ounce of compassion in your fickle heart, you'll let me walk out this door and out of your life. Because I can't handle an affair with you."

Although she was too blinded by tears to see his expression clearly, she felt the silent inspection of his gaze. Rome exhaled a long breath and withdrew his hand from the door.

"Very well," he agreed. "But I'll walk you to your car."

Lexie held the door ajar, her eyes tightly closed as a shaft of pure pain stabbed her. "Don't waste any gestures of gallantry on me, Rome," she demanded tightly.

"Dammit, Lexie, it's night," he hurled at her, "and it's a city street out there. If you want to get out of my life, at least let me see that you get out of it safely!"

She choked out, "Have it your way," and jerked the door open.

It seemed the longest walk Lexie had ever taken—with Rome walking at her side, not touching her—and her heart wanting to burst with each step. She missed seeing the curb and stumbled, but she recovered quickly and avoided Rome's attempt to steady her with his hand.

Without glancing at him she unlocked the car door and opened it. "Goodbye," she mumbled, and slid behind the wheel.

"I'll be seeing you."

It was just a parting phrase but if Lexie could help it, she was going to see that it never came true. Or, at least, not for a very long time.

The following Monday around midmorning, Lexie found herself gravitating to Shari's semiprivate office to have coffee with the columnist and Ginger. It was an unconscious attempt to avoid being alone with her thoughts, which invariably swung to Rome. As long as she was surrounded by work or people, the ache inside didn't seem as intense. She did little of the talking, but with Ginger around, it didn't matter.

"Don't you just love this outfit?" The question was directed at Shari as Ginger did a pirouette. Lace trimmed the snug-fitting denim jeans she wore, as well as the denim vest.

"It's definitely you, my dear," Shari agreed with a trace of dryness. A tiny smile touched Lexie's mouth. With her old-fashioned, Midwestern charm, the outfit did seem to match Ginger's personality.

"We were walking by this store, and I saw it in the window," Ginger explained excitedly. "I showed it to Bob and said 'isn't it pretty.' He asked me if I wanted it. I said sure, and he walked right in and bought it for me, just like that." She snapped her fingers.

"And I suppose you were properly grateful," Shari murmured suggestively.

Ginger blushed. "Who wouldn't be? It's beautiful. I love it."

"I'm sure he counted on that," Lexie inserted in a sudden surge of bitterness at the selfish motives of men.

Her roommate darted her an angry, resentful glance. "You're just upset because—" she stopped and made a quick change of the sentence ending "—you don't have anybody to buy you presents."

But Lexie knew something about Rome had been on the tip of Ginger's tongue. She felt her muscles tense and wondered if the astute columnist was reading between the lines. She stole a sideways glance at Shari. She had been watching Lexie, although now her gaze was swinging lazily to Ginger.

"Lexie and I are in the same boat there, but your love life seems to be sailing right along," she commented. "Speaking about love life, Rome Lockwood seems to have dropped out of circulation. You wouldn't know anything about that, would you, Lexie?"

"Me?" She pretended surprise but didn't know how successful she was. "Why should I?"

"I don't know," Shari said with a little shrug. "It was just an idea I had."

"You're flogging a dead horse," Lexie murmured and sipped at the coffee in her Styrofoam cup.

"Hey, Lexie!" Gary Dunbar paused in the opening to the office. "You're being paged for a phone call. What are you doing Friday night?"

"Nothing," she answered. Her eagerness was more

for Shari's benefit than a desire to spend the evening with Gary.

"We'll go to a movie or something," he suggested.

"Fine," Lexie agreed.

"Around seven then." He started to retreat, then reminded her, "Don't forget that phone call."

"Do you want me to have it transferred here?" the columnist asked as Lexie started to rise from her chair.

"Why don't you," she agreed. "I'll probably need some paper and a pencil. Can you spare some?"

"Right there." Shari tossed her a notebook and picked up the telephone, calling the switchboard to have the phone call transferred to her extension. "Who's calling please?" she asked. Her eyes glinted at the answer and she handed the phone to Lexie. "Rome Lockwood for you, Lexie. And you have nothing to do with him being out of circulation," she mocked.

Lexie's stomach tied itself into knots as she reached for the telephone receiver. She silently cursed the listless attitude that had prompted her to take the call here instead of her own desk. Alone, she could have hung up on him or refused to take the call. But with Shari Sullivan looking on and listening, she didn't dare.

"Lexie Templeton here." Miraculously her voice had no nervous tremor.

"Lexie, it's Rome," he identified himself needlessly. The familiar pitch of his voice reached across the distance to disturb the beat of her heart.

"What a surprise," she murmured and heard the faint thread of sarcasm sewn into the words.

"Is it?" Rome mocked dryly. "I've had time to think over what you said Saturday night. I'd like you to have dinner with me on Friday. My family is giving a party for some friends that night, and I'd like you to—"

"A party," Lexie interrupted with false brightness. "I'm flattered that you thought of me, but it really isn't my line. You really should speak to the society editor. Would you like me to connect you?"

"That isn't what I want at all, and you damn well know it!" Rome's voice was low and angry at her deliberate obtuseness. He didn't know that it had been mostly for Shari's benefit.

"I'm sorry. The...there isn't any way I can help you." Why did she have to stammer like a silly schoolgirl, Lexie railed inwardly.

She heard him swearing under his breath. "Is it so much to ask that I want to see you again?" he demanded.

"I'm afraid it is," she insisted. "Goodbye, Mr. Lockwood."

Lexie hung up the phone before he could say something that might change her mind. She felt ashen and drained, but there was still Shari to be faced.

"What was he calling about?" the columnist asked. "Was there some party he wanted you to attend?"

"Yes." Lexie took a drink of her coffee, trying to wash down the lump in her throat. "His parents are having a dinner party. He seemed to think the paper might find it newsworthy." She made a show of glancing at her watch. "I'd better run." She started for the door. "Maybe you'll be covering the party, Shari. Nothing the Lockwood's do would ever be of interest to me."

WITHIN A WEEK, Lexie had cause to contradict those thoughts as she sat at her desk listening to Mike explain her day's assignment—that of covering the arrival and activities of a visiting foreign dignitary.

"Officially he's here on an unofficial visit to see his old friends, the Lockwoods. He'll be staying at their home in Marblehead. But unofficially—" Mike paused to give his seeming double-talk importance, "—rumor is it's a cover-up for a secret State meeting. I want you to stick to his party like glue. Follow him into the men's john if you have to."

"I don't think I can do it," Lexie protested.

"The men's john was an exaggeration," Mike frowned impatiently. "His plane arrives...."

"No, I mean, I don't think I can cover the story." There was only one Lockwood family in Boston and that was Rome's.

"Why?" he demanded gruffly.

"Because...." But Lexie couldn't think of a reason that she wanted to tell him.

Mike took one look at her flushed cheeks and grimly guessed, "Lockwood. What exactly happened on your date that you were so mum about? I suppose you slapped his face or pulled some equally stupid female trick."

"I'd rather you find somebody else to take this assignment." How in the world could she explain?

"You would, would you?"

"If you don't mind, I'd really appreciate it," Lexie offered hopefully.

"It so happens that I do mind. This assignment is yours and as a professional, you're going to accept it." His stern demeanor weakened slightly at the strained white look on her face. "Besides, I don't have anyone else qualified to cover it." It was the best Mike could do for an apology and his mouth thinned in sympathy before he moved away from her desk.

Mac the photographer had drawn the assignment along with Lexie. Together they went to Logan International Airport to be on hand for the arrival. As Lexie had guessed, Rome was there with an older couple whom she presumed to be his parents. Since it was an unofficial visit and not designed to be a media event, the press was kept away from the welcoming party.

But Lexie was near enough—too near, her pulse felt—to notice Rome's similarities to his parents. His mother was a dark, vivacious woman and Lexie realized it was from her that Rome had inherited his coloring. It was from his father that he received his striking good looks—tall and masculine. Her statement the other night that Rome would age with character and experience was borne out in his father. The man was still handsome enough to warrant the pursuit of women.

When the European dignitary—Lexie had to check her notes to recall his name, Edmond Martineau—departed from his private jet, he was accompanied by a small entourage, and Lexie suspected that Mike had cause to believe there was more to the visit than had been released.

"Wow!" Mac whistled under his breath. "Would you get a load of her!"

Jealousy twisted through Lexie at the sight of the woman coming into their view. Stunning, chic as only the French can be, sophisticated to the bone, the petite brunette in her designer suit glided forward to be at

Edmond Martineau's side as he greeted the Lock-woods.

"The next question is," Mac murmured in an aside, "is she his daughter, his wife, or his mistress?"

When the woman kissed and clung to Rome's arm, looking up at him with a coyly flirtatious smile, Lexie wanted to die. Rome seemed to be not only enjoying the attention but also encouraging it, that male charm and breathtaking smile directed at the woman at his side. Lexie had known seeing him again was going to be difficult but she hadn't realized it would be so painful.

Security kept the press away from the initial exchange, allowing them only to witness it at a distance. It soon became apparent that they were not going to be allowed to question Edmond Martineau about his visit nor was he going to give them any statement before he left the airport. They had all waited for nothing. Lexie heard the disgruntled mutterings from the other reporters, but they made little impression.

As Rome and his party started to make their way to a private lounge, Mac grumbled to Lexie, "We're not coming away from this empty-handed. Come on." He grabbed her hand and pulled her behind him as he shouldered his way as close as he could get. "Hey, Rome!" he shouted, lifting his camera high over his head. "How about a letting us have a picture?"

Rome sent a cursory glance over his shoulder in Mac's direction. His gaze lingered for a scant second on Lexie's red gold hair. She knew he had to have recognized her, but he didn't pause, continuing with his party to the private lounge. Her heart went dead.

A slow exodus of reporters began. The general consensus seemed to be that they would have a better chance when the party went to get in the waiting cars. Lexie was eager to leave, but Mac kept a firm clasp on her hand.

"The others..." she started to protest.

"We're going to wait here." There was a shrewd gleam in his eye as he stared at the closed door. "I've got a hunch and I'm betting that I'm right."

Lexie glanced at the door with an apprehensive frown just as it opened. The man who stepped out had been part of the arriving Martineau entourage.

He looked at her and said in a faintly accented voice, "Miss Templeton? Please come in."

She was frozen, but Mac wasn't. "I knew it!" he breathed in satisfaction, and pushed her ahead of him to the door.

The entire party was seated in the lounge: Edmond Martineau, the brunette, half a dozen aides and embassy officials, Rome's parents and Rome. All looked up when Lexie and Mac entered the lounge, but it was only Rome that Lexie saw. Her legs felt like two sticks of quivering jelly beneath her.

His gaze held nothing for her; neither warm nor cold it was merely different. He stepped forward at their approach, his smile minus the devastation it was capable of producing.

"Mr. Martineau has consented to answer a few questions and be photographed," Rome announced quietly.

"Terrific," Mac was enthusiastic, but Lexie could only nod.

Rome turned and walked beside her to the chair where his family's important guest was seated. Edmond Martineau rose smiling widely at Lexie. Before Rome could make the formal introductions, Martineau sent him a twinkling glance. "Now I understand why you asked this favor of me, Rome. She is a very beautiful lady."

"Thank you," Lexie murmured at the compliment, too self-conscious to derive any pleasure from it.

There was an awkward moment when Rome introduced her, his mother piping up with, "The Miss Templeton?"

"The one and only," Rome had assured her dryly, using the same identifying words Lexie herself had once used. Lexie guessed from his mother's suddenly intent look that she had recognized Lexie's name from Shari's column.

The introduction ascertained one thing; the brunette was Martineau's daughter, Claudine. Her interest in Rome was even more apparent with Lexie looking on.

With the introductions over, it was time to begin the questions. Lexie began by asking what was expected of her—the reason of his visit, et cetera—and received the expected answer—to visit old friends, the Lockwoods. Edmond Martineau had been a classmate of Rome's father at Harvard while taking part in a foreign-exchange program, and they had remained close friends ever since, although it had been many years since Martineau had paid them a visit.

When Lexie asked, "When will you be meeting with the representatives from the State Department?" a fine tension crackled through the room.

It was perhaps only a second or two before Martineau laughed and denied, "This is purely a social visit. Miss Templeton—a few restful days with my old friends and a chance for my daughter to see the picturesque city of Boston."

"Of course; my mistake." Lexie smiled wanly, aware of the rapier thrust of Rome's gaze piercing into her. She turned away. "Mac? Would you like to get the rest of your pictures?"

She would have faded quietly into the wall while Mac snapped the rest of his photographs, but Rome didn't permit it, drifting to her side while Mac took pictures of Martineau and his daughter. Lexie tried to pretend he wasn't there, which was ridiculous, because every nerve in her body screamed with his presence.

"When we leave the airport," said Rome, "we will be taking Miss Martineau on a tour of some of Boston's historic points. Would you like to accompany us?"

Mac's hearing was exceptional because it was he who answered, "You bet we would!"

Lexie hesitated. With Mike's admonition to both of them to stick with Martineau until they had got to the bottom of his visit, it was impossible for Lexie to refuse this chance.

"It's kind of you to offer," she accepted stiffly.

"Not kind, Lexie. Not kind at all." Rome reply was low and sardonic, meant only for her to hear.

And there was no kindness in it, only pain.

They made the Freedom Trail tour of Boston, starting out at Christ Church or, as it is better known, Old North Church, where two lanterns were hung in its steeple in 1775 to signal that the British were coming "by sea." From there they moved on to Paul Revere's house, the oldest standing structure in downtown Boston, past a statue of Samuel Adams to Faneuil Hall, the "Cradle of Liberty," and then made a stop at the Boston Massacre site, by the Old State House, seat of the Colonial government.

At every place Lexie was forced to watch Rome escorting the beautiful Claudine, explaining the historic significance to her and laughing at her comments. She should have taken advantage of the situation to question Edmond Martineau more closely but she hadn't the heart for it. It seemed so terribly unimportant.

She stared into the window of the Old Corner Bookstore, seeing her strained features in its indistinct reflection. There was no feeling of history there for her, no thought that once the literary greats such as Emerson, Hawthorne and Holmes had possibly looked in the very same window when they had made it their meeting place and made Boston "the Athens of America."

Another reflection joined hers in the glass pane and Lexie stiffened. A further glance saw none of the others in the party, only Rome standing alone behind her. She knew she couldn't risk a personal discussion. She had long ago discovered that when you can't defend you should attack.

She turned. "I thought you told me that your family made it a rule not to become actively involved in politics."

"We don't become involved, and certainly not on an international level," Rome denied again.

She felt the dissection of his gaze, studying, penetrating, trying to see through her brittle mask. "And Mr. Martineau's visit?"

"His visit is exactly what he claims it to be—a reunion of friends."

"There's more to it than that," Lexie insisted.

"Is that why you were at the airport? And why you came along with us?"

"Of course—it's my assignment. I wouldn't be here otherwise." And that was the absolute truth.

"I see." Black shutters seemed to close over his eyes.

"I'm glad you do." She looked away. Where was Mac? No doubt with the beautiful Claudine.

"You're right. There is more to Martineau's visit than just the reunion," Rome said unexpectedly, and Lexie stared at him, surprised that he should suddenly admit it. "Within the next forty-eight hours it will officially be announced that he's been invited to the White House to meet with the Secretary of State."

"Then this is all a cover-up?"

"No. His visit to my parents has simply precipitated the invitation."

"If what you're saying is true, then why all the secrecy?" Lexie was skeptical.

Rome seemed not to care whether she believed him or not. "As I understand, it's a matter of diplomacy. Until the invitation is officially issued, Edmond doesn't acknowledge its existence. You should be more familiar with such things than I."

Frowning, she looked away. There was enough logic in his answer for her to believe him. Now she wondered what his motive was in telling her.

"Why have you told me?" she demanded, unable to come up with a reason on her own.

There was an arrogant glitter in his look. "It's in the way of a reward, I suppose. After the lengths you've gone to carry out your assignment I wouldn't like to see you report back with nothing."

Lexie would have questioned him further to test that cynical mockery in his voice but Martineau and his daughter and Rome's parents came around the corner of the building. And her chance was gone.

She heard them say that the Old South Meeting House, where the Boston Tea Party was launched, was their next stop. Claudine Martineau locked her hands possessively on Rome's elbow and Lexie knew she could endure no more of seeing them together. Mac was trailing the group, trying to juggle camera film and lenses. She led him aside.

"This is where we leave," Lexie told him.

"But...." He cast a protesting look at the disappearing group.

"We have our story. Now let's get back to the paper," she insisted as though she was certain she had a story. When she related it to Mike at the office, she downplayed its authenticity and avoided naming the person who had given her the information.

"What about your source?" Mike asked.

"I don't know how reliable he is," she admitted.

"It's Rome Lockwood, that's who it is," Mac declared from his perch on the edge of Mike's desk. "I tell ya, Mike, we've got ourselves an exclusive! Rome's the one responsible for getting us invited along. Lexie won't admit he gave her the information, but they were off by themselves talking and right afterward she tells me we're heading back to the office. It has to be him."

"Lockwood, huh?" Mike eyed her, remembering her unwillingness to take the assignment because of Rome. "Do you think he might be feeding you false information to make you look like a fool?"

"He's trying to make points with her," the photographer inserted.

Lexie stuck to her story. "As I said, I don't know

how reliable my source is. But I do know that Edmond Martineau isn't going to let anything slip. Keeping tabs on him will be a waste of time."

Mike considered the problem for a minute. "It will be announced within forty-eight hours, you say?"

"Yes," she nodded.

"Shari Sullivan tells me the Lockwoods are throwing a big dinner party for Martineau on Friday night—the forty-eight hours you were saying—and it would be the perfect opportunity to make the announcement." He seemed to be speaking his thoughts aloud, for he suddenly took a deep breath and glanced at them both. "I have a few old connections in the State Department. If I get even a hint of verification, we'll run your story on Friday morning, Lex."

She didn't feel any sense of elation at the news.

CHAPTER EIGHT

"THAT'S GREAT NEWS, Mike," Lexie said to the man standing in front of her desk. She should have been more elated than she was by his announcement. Instead her enthusiasm was forced.

"My connections at the State Department tried to be closemouthed about Martineau's visit. But after I reminded them of the favors they owed me, they finally confirmed your story," he elaborated, managing a smug smile despite the cigarette dangling out of his mouth.

"I'm glad to hear it," she lied again.

"You'd better get in gear and get the story written up if you want your by-line to make the front page on Friday morning," Mike ordered. "You did a helluva job, Lexie. Which proves, I guess, that it pays to know the right people."

"I suppose," she nodded, concealing a sigh.

Mac, the photographer, had convinced Mike that she had used her persuasive powers on Rome to get the admission from him. Mike thought she had wheedled the information from him like any good reporter. But Lexie knew that the story had been handed to her on a platter. So Mike's announcement gave her no satisfaction.

"You suppose?" he retorted with a snort. "We'll

break the story twenty-four hours before any other paper in town, and you suppose it pays to know the right people?''

"I was using your words, Mike," she reminded him and reached to insert a piece of paper in her typewriter.

"Humphh." The ashes from his cigarette fell on her desk. He brushed them to the floor with his broad, flat hand. "It doesn't matter how you got the story. Everybody in the trade is going to sit up and take notice of you when you show up at that dinner party tomorrow night."

"The dinner party?" Lexie swiveled her chair toward him. "There's no need for me to attend that. I've already got the story."

"You've got the advance story. Now you've got to cover the official announcement, which should be made at this shindig," Mike said. "You can cover that and whatever else develops out of it."

"No." She couldn't do it. She couldn't face Rome again. "Let somebody else go. It's just routine from here on."

"What are you?" Placing his hands on her desk, he leaned across it to emphasize his words. "A reporter? Or a glory-hunting, headline seeker?"

"I'm a reporter," Lexie insisted defensively.

"Are you sure?" he persisted. "Maybe you've fallen in love with seeing your name in print. Is that why you let Sullivan put all those quotes from you about Lockwood in her column? You've gained a little notoriety, and now you think you're too good to cover routine stuff, is that it?"

"No," she denied. "It just so happens that I have a date Friday night."

"With whom?" Mike wanted to know, leaning closer and breathing cigarette smoke from his mouth like dragon's fire.

"Gary Dunbar. He works in features," Lexie answered.

Mike rolled the cigarette to the other side of his mouth, his teeth clamping onto the end of it. "Break it," he ordered.

"I don't want to break my date."

"All right." He straightened and turned to bark, "Dunbar! Somebody get me Dunbar on the double!"

"What are you doing!" Lexie demanded and guessed that her editor intended to throw his weight around by ordering Gary to break the date. "So help me, Mike, if you—"

"Just shut up, Lexie, and let me handle this." His gruff retort sliced off her futile and powerless threat. There wasn't any more time to argue as Gary came rushing toward them.

"You wanted to see me, Mr. Farragut?" he asked nervously.

"Lexie tells me the two of you have a heavy date tomorrow night." The statement sounded like an accusation.

Gary looked momentarily flustered. "Yes, we have a date tomorrow night." He avoided using the adjective "heavy" as he darted a faintly embarrassed glance at Lexie.

"Where are you going?" Mike wanted to know, his hands on his hips in challenge.

"Well, I...uh...." Gary quailed under glowering demand of the editor, then continued, "There's a new Fonda movie premiering tomorrow night. Stan, over in movie reviews, gave me a couple of free tickets. I thought Lexie and I might go to see it.''

"Wrong!" Mike barked. "You are going with Lexie to a dinner party the Lockwood's are giving tomorrow night for Edmond Martineau. Okay?" It wasn't really a question of Gary agreeing, not as far as Mike was concerned. It was more of a dare to disagree. "Lexie is covering the event for the paper."

"Sure. Fine. That's all right with me." Gary practically fell all over himself in his hurry to agree with the change of plans. Only at the last second did he think to consult Lexie. "It will be okay, won't it, Lexie?"

It seemed she had as little choice as Gary did. He wouldn't be a very adequate shield against Rome, but he was better than none. Since she had to go to the dinner party, she'd rather attend with an escort in tow.

"As long as you don't mind, it's fine with me," she agreed with only a trace of grimness.

"I don't mind," he assured her.

"Then it's all settled," Mike declared, glancing at Lexie to see if she intended to argue the point any further.

She took a deep breath and nodded, "It's all settled."

"Good." He chewed on the end of his cigarette. "Get back to whatever you were doing Dunbar," he ordered gruffly. "And you," he said squinty gaze sliding to Lexie, "get busy on that story. I want it on my desk in half an hour."

She turned her swivel chair to face the typewriter and rolled the paper through the carriage cylinder. Gary was already hustling back to his desk. Mike stayed until he saw the first typewriter key being struck.

As THEY WALKED down the plush hotel corridor to the banquet room rented for the occasion, Gary's skittish gaze darted over the guests making their way to the same destination. They were all dressed to the teeth, the men in black-tie and the women in gowns and adorned with jewelry. Gary cleared his throat nervously and adjusted his brown-striped tie.

"You could have given me a hint about what I was letting myself in for tonight," he whispered to Lexie. "I could have rented something formal."

"Don't worry. We're reporters. We're supposed to look conspicuous so no one will blab any secrets, mistaking us for one of them," she answered.

The butterflies in her stomach had nothing to do with her casual state of dress. They came from a mixture of anticipation and apprehension at seeing Rome again. Against her better judgment, she had allowed Mike to maneuver her into this.

It wasn't any use pretending she did it just to keep her job, but it provided the perfect excuse.

At the doorway to the banquet room, they were stopped. Lexie showed the man her press card as her gaze skimmed the already crowded room for a glimpse of Rome. Her initial sweep didn't find him. A crazy mixture of disappointment and relief quivered through her as they stepped into the room.

"There's the queen bee herself, Shari Sullivan," Gary remarked in the direction of the stunning, if aging, blond columnist. "Somebody must have forgotten to tell her about the unwritten code of dress for journalists."

Lexie's gaze ran admiringly over the elegant chiffon cocktail dress Shari was wearing. It was in marked contrast to the midnight-blue tailored suit Lexie wore. The manly cut of her skirt and jacket was alleviated by the ruffled white blouse she wore and the way the deep blue of the material drew attention to the aquamarine color of her eyes.

"Columnists don't fall in the same category as we lowly reporters," Lexie explained. "They want to appear the equal of those around them—or better."

"That's how they persuade people to tell their secrets, I suppose," Gary grinned.

"That's the idea," she agreed, a ghost of a smile touching her tense features.

Shari happened to glance their way and saw them standing near the outer wall of the room. She excused herself to the couple with whom she was chatting and made her way toward them.

"Hello, Shari," Lexie greeted her. "You look lovely tonight."

The columnist unconsciously preened at the compliment. "Thank you," she smiled. "What brings you here? I thought you said once that the Lockwoods weren't newsworthy."

"They aren't," Lexie countered the slight dig. "But Edmond Martineau is."

"And eligible, too," the columnist observed, turning so she could look toward the center of the room without being obvious. "When he said *bon soir* to me in that gorgeous French accent, I wanted to melt like an éclair in the July sun. He's had that effect on every woman in the room, married or single."

The crowd of people seemed to part to give Lexie an unobstructed view of the guest of honor. But it was the tall, raven-haired man beside him who captured her attention. When that dark head bent to catch the comment of the chic brunette on his arm, a jealous bile seemed to fill Lexie's mouth.

"Everyone is whispering about Rome and the Martineau girl. They've been practically inseparable since she arrived," Shari informed Lexie with deliberate insensitivity. "Have you noticed the way she clings to Rome as though he were her security blanket?"

Lexie's teeth seemed welded together, hardening the line of her jaw. "Maybe she's the reason he's been out of circulation lately." Lexie's offhand comment was coated with bitterness.

Shari's bright eyes glittered with triumph as her arrow found its target. "You had your chance, darling," she reminded Lexie.

"Chance at what?" Lexie retorted angrily. "I've outgrown merry-go-rounds."

"Gary must be relieved to know that." Shari glanced at Lexie's male companion. "I presume you're accompanying Lexie merely as her escort. Or did Features assign you to do a story on tonight's festivities?"

"No, I'm just here with Lexie," he admitted. "We had a date tonight, and Mike Farragut just chose the place we were going." Gary laughed as if he had made a joke, but Lexie couldn't find anything about the arrangement that was very funny.

"When will they be shooing the reporters out?" Lexie changed the subject.

"Hors d'oeuvres and cocktails are being served until eight-thirty," Shari replied. "Dinner won't be until nine, a more continental hour. I would imagine they'll permit the reporters to remain until the cocktail hour is over. Of course, I'll be staying for the whole affair.''

"Of course," Lexie murmured caustically. Personally she wanted to leave now. The sight of Rome with the elegant Claudine was tearing her apart.

"You'll never learn anything standing here, darling," Shari insisted. "All the action is over by the cocktail bar. Shall we wander over and help ourselves to some of the refreshments?''

"That sounds like a good idea." Gary was more than willing to follow someone else's lead. All of this was out of his sphere of experience.

They had to cross the full width of the room to reach the bar. It was the first time in her life that Lexie could ever remember wanting to be a wallflower.

Her nervous stomach could not tolerate the thought of alcohol or food. The bartender lifted an eyebrow when she ordered a soft drink, but filled it without comment.

She had barely stepped away when she heard Rome's familiar voice inquire, "What would you like, Claudine?'' Tremors of awareness quaked through her at how close he stood to her.

A feather-soft voice responded, "Some white wine, *s'il vous plaît*.'' The English words were spoken with a delightful French accent.

Lexie couldn't help turning to look at them as Rome gave the bartender their order. Her gaze was met by a pair of brown eyes as soft as the voice of their owner. Recognition was instant.

"Miss Templeton, it's a pleasure to see you again," Claudine Martineau declared. The tone of her voice always seemed to be barely above a whisper. It enhanced the aura of fragility her petiteness conveyed and carried through the impression of youthful innocence despite her overall elegance.

To make matters worse, as far as Lexie was concerned, the phrase sounded sincere. It was impossible to make a caustic response.

"Thank you, Miss Martineau." The words were stiff, but at least they weren't tinged with sarcasm.

"I enjoyed so much the tour of your city the other day," the brunette continued. "Rome had told me many things about it." At that moment, Rome returned to her side and handed her a glass of wine. "It was all that you said it would be, *chérie*," Claudine told him.

"I'm glad." The smile disappeared from his mouth when he glanced at Lexie, all expression leaving his face. "How are you, Miss Templeton?"

The question was so impersonal, so distant, that she wanted to scream. More than that, she wanted to take the wine glass from Claudine and spill the contents all over her designer gown. She wanted to do anything that would dim the woman's attraction in Rome's eyes. But her fingers curled more tightly around her own glass as she held her temper.

"Fine, thank you, Mr. Lockwood." The boiling heat of her frustration simmered in her voice.

Gary politely made his way through the crowd to reach Lexie. "Whew, I almost lost you in the crowd," he laughed self-consciously. "Did you get your drink?"

"Yes."

"Good. I—" He saw Rome standing there and seemed to redden. "Hello, Mr. Lockwood."

"Hello. You have the advantage on me. I'm afraid I don't know your name." The black gaze flickered arrogantly to Lexie, demanding an introduction.

"This is Gary Dunbar," she identified her escort, then reversed the introductions. "Mr. Lockwood you know, and this is Mademoiselle Claudine Martineau, Edmond Martineau's daughter."

"It is a pleasure, *m'sier*." The woman offered Gary her hand.

"The pleasure is all mine, *mamselle*." He awkwardly attempted to kiss the back of her hand in the continental fashion.

He was so plainly fascinated and awed by this stunning creature from France that he was falling all over himself trying to impress her. Lexie felt sorry for him, and also defensive, especially when she saw the derisive look Rome gave him.

"You two are here together tonight, no?" Claudine asked, wide-eyed.

Lexie began to realize what allure the woman's soft tone had. It invited a person to lean closer. Lexie doubted that there was a man in the room who didn't enjoy that.

"No, that is, yes, we came together," Gary admitted.

"Gary is also a reporter?" Claudine glanced at Lexie for confirmation.

"Yes," she nodded, aware of Rome's black gaze watching her trying to avoid to meeting it. A pulse was racing wildly in her throat, the sound of it pounding in her ears.

"It is convenient that he works for your newspaper," the woman commented.

"We work for the same newspaper. It's hardly mine," Lexie corrected, not wanting to convey the impression that she was anything more than a reporter.

"It must be fascinating work," Claudine insisted. "It is certain that you meet many interesting people."

"I do," Gary assured her. "I enjoy my work tremendously. I would like to travel more than I do, see some of the world, but you can't have everything."

"Ah, yes, travel," the woman nodded. "Men seem to be born with a wish to travel. Me, I am a 'keep-at-home.'"

"Stay-at-home," Rome corrected her idiom.

Claudine laughed at her own mistake. It reminded Lexie of the soft tinkling sound of silver bells, and Gary seemed enraptured by it. There was warmth in Rome's look, too, when he gazed at the woman whose petite frame came no higher than his shoulder. The delicate laugh irritated Lexie.

"Rome knows me so well," Claudine smiled. "He even knows what I mean when it isn't what I say."

"Lexie mentioned that your families are very close," Gary remarked.

"*C'est vrai*. It is true. Rome's papa and mine are very close, like brothers," the brunette explained. A light danced in her eyes as her gaze swept to Rome through naturally long lashes. "Rome has known me since I was an *enfant*."

"Thank heavens, you aren't an infant anymore," he mocked.

"When I was younger, I had a—how do you say it—a crush on Rome," confided Claudine, smiling at Rome with shared memories. "I followed him around like a puppy dog."

"And now?" Shari Sullivan spoke from behind Lexie, having unobtrusively joined the group. "Have you managed to snare Rome Lockwood?"

"*Pardon?* Snare?" Claudine repeated the word with a puzzled and blank look.

Shari rephrased the question. "Is there a romance between the two of you?"

Lexie wanted to push her way out of the group before Claudine answered, but she was hemmed in to the point where it was impossible. She somehow managed to control the almost overwhelming sensation of panic.

"Claudine, may I introduce Shari Sullivan," Rome interrupted before his companion could respond to Shari's question. "She has a society column."

"For the same newspaper as Miss Templeton?" Claudine asked.

"Yes," Shari admitted.

"Is there no one at the shop to print the newspaper?" Claudine jested. "Are you all here tonight?"

"Not quite," the columnist responded dryly, aware that it was all a ploy to avoid a direct answer to her question.

"As I was—"

"To answer your previous question, Miss Sullivan," Rome interrupted smoothly, "Claudine and I are—" his pause was deliberate "—just good friends."

"*Oui,*" Claudine agreed with a bright smile. "We are good friends."

Lexie felt sick. Good friends. It was the term so often used to hide a deeper relationship. Seeing them together, looking into each other's eyes, she could well imagine that the term intimated just that.

"I am sure you regret your visit is such a short one,"

Shari was saying. "I believe you are leaving the day after tomorrow. You've barely had time to see your friend, what with the tour of Boston and the reception tonight."

"The dinner tonight is necessary in order to meet everyone." Claudine didn't express any regret for the multitude of people of the party. "Tomorrow we'll have a quiet evening with just our two families." A manicured hand touched Rome's sleeve as Claudine glanced beyond them through the throng of people. "Look, *chérie*. Papa is about to propose a toast. Your mama and papa are there, too. Perhaps we should join them."

Rome nodded, encompassing them all in a look. "Excuse us, please."

As he shouldered a path through the crowd, protectively drawing the petite French woman along with him, Lexie felt the sickening wave of nausea pass. More than anything she wanted to sit down. Her knees had begun to tremble until she wondered how much longer they would support her.

"Come on." Shari's gaze had not left the departing couple, her expression hardening with purpose. "Let's find out what's going on. I want a closer look."

As she started forward, Gary automatically followed. Lexie was caught in the middle and swept along with them. When she was able to stop, she found herself on the inner ring of a semicircle around the host family and their guests of honor. Edmond Martineau raised his glass in a toast.

"To my friends, the Lockwoods. May our visits be more frequent in the future." As he sipped from his glass, others did likewise.

There was a hush in the room while everyone, the reporters especially, waited for another announcement. It was several seconds before they began to realize nothing more was forthcoming.

A reporter from a competitive newspaper spoke up. "Excuse me. Were the Lockwoods your only reason for visiting the United States at this time, Mr. Martineau?"

With a stricken look, Lexie glanced at Rome. What if the information he'd given her was wrong? Mike said he had confirmed it, but—

"Perhaps," Edmond Martineau paused, drawing Lexie's gaze. His eyes twinkled brightly back at her. "Perhaps, you should put the question to Miss Templeton." An amused murmur ran through the crowd. "She claims to know a great deal about my reasons for coming to your country."

She swallowed once and tried to find her voice. "Isn't it true that when you leave here Sunday, you will be flying to Washington, D.C.?"

Edmond Martineau glanced around the room and lifted his hand in a Gallic gesture. "How can I, a Frenchman, deny a beautiful lady the confirmation she seeks? It is true. I fly to Washington where I will meet with members of your State Department."

Rome hadn't lied to her. Her gaze swung back to him in relief, but he was looking at her with almost savage contempt. The statement by Martineau had prompted a flurry of questions from the other reporters. As they rushed forward to vie for his attention, Lexie allowed them to close around her and force her into the background. She felt sick and cold, and must have looked worse. Gary frowned at her with concern.

"Are you all right Lexie?"

"No." She didn't lie. "I don't feel very well, Gary. Would you mind taking me home?"

"No, I don't mind," he assured her and curved an arm around her waist to escort her out of the room.

"I'm sorry to spoil the evening this way," she apologized once they were in the car.

"Hey, it's all right," He shrugged. "I understand."

"I'll get over it." Lexie meant Rome, and knew it wasn't going to be easy.

SATURDAY NIGHT the telephone rang while Lexie was in the bathtub. Her first inclination was to let it ring, but common sense drove her out of the bubbly water. It might be an important call. She quickly wrapped a bath towel around her as she hurried into the living room.

"Hello." Her voice sounded strained even to her own ears.

"Hi, let me speak to Carla," a bright female voice requested.

"You must have the wrong number. There isn't anyone here by that name," Lexie replied.

"Are you sure? This is the number she gave me."

"Well, it's the wrong one."

"Is this 555-4121?" the voice demanded.

"No."

"Sorry." The line clicked dead.

Retracing her watery trail to the bathroom, Lexie found the bubbles had all dissipated and the bathwater was tepid. Her skin was already dry so there was little use for the towel wrapped around her. She unwound it and slipped on her quilted housecoat, using the towel to mop up her wet footprints from the floor.

Hanging the damp towel on a rack, she wandered into the small living room. The apartment seemed so silent and empty. Ginger was out with Bob again and Lexie was alone. It wasn't a night when she wanted to be alone. But then was any night? She wouldn't admit the real reason she felt so empty and lonely. She picked up a book and put it back down.

There was a knock at the apartment door. Lexie stared at it wondering who would be visiting at this late hour. Not for the first time she wished the door had a peephole as she moved to answer the knock. She slipped the night chain securely in place and opened the door the few inches the chain permitted.

"Hello, Lexie." Rome stood outside, resplendent in black-tie evening wear.

"What are you doing here?" she breathed, certain he would vanish any second.

There was a trace of his old teasing mockery when he spoke, "I thought it was obvious. I came to see you. May I come in?"

"No." Her answer was abrupt as she recovered her initial surprise. "I don't want to see you."

"I want to talk to you, Lexie."

"I think I've heard that line before," she said bitterly.

His mouth straightened. "I give you my word, Lexie. We'll talk. That's all."

She started to close the door without answering him, but his hand slipped into the opening to stop her. Lexie wondered if the chain would hold if Rome tried to force his way in. It suddenly didn't look very substantial.

"Shut the door if you want," Rome told her. "I can

talk loudly enough for you to hear me, even through a closed door. But either way, Lexie, you're going to listen to me.''

He removed his hand from the door. Lexie closed it, hesitated, then slipped off the chain. Rome was capable of doing exactly what he said, and she didn't want that type of discussion carried on in a public hallway. She opened the door for him to enter and walked away.

"I thought you were giving a big important party for the Martineaus tonight," she commented.

"I'm not. My parents are." At her pointed glance at his formal attire, Rome added, "I put in an appearance and left."

"Why are you here?" Lexie's nerves were as charged as a high-voltage wire. They stood in the center of the small room, facing each other.

"I saw the article in this morning's paper."

"Have you come to congratulate me? Or to collect your due?" she hurled. "I should have known you had some devious reason for telling me. Now that your information gave me a scoop, you expect me to be suitably grateful. Well, I'm sorry, but your word wasn't good enough. We confirmed the information through other sources. Any credit I owe you is strictly negligible."

"I didn't come to collect any imaginary debt," corrected Rome.

"Didn't you?"

"No. I told you why I came. We have to talk," he declared again.

"And I told you I didn't want to become involved with you. I don't even want to see you." Which was a lie. Her eyes were drinking in the sight of him, so formidably male.

"That seems to be my problem. You see, I've discovered that I want to see you again while you still claim that you don't want to see me. How do you suppose I can solve that?"

"I don't know." Lexie pivoted away in agitation. "It's your problem, isn't it?"

"Can't we compromise?"

"Can't I change my mind, is what you mean," she retorted. "Why don't you go back to your party? I'm sure Claudine can offer you a solution."

"Were you jealous?" Rome taunted. "I hope so. I hope you were miserable."

Lexie whirled to face him. "Is that why you singled Mac and me out from all the others at the airport? Why you invited us along on the tour? So I'd have to watch you with her?"

"I had so many reasons for inviting you along that I doubt if I can remember them all." There were troubled, black storm clouds in his eyes and Lexie's breath caught at his answer. "When I saw you standing out like a beacon light in the crowd of reporters, I knew I had to be near you again. And I was willing to use whatever means I had at hand to accomplish it—even if it included trading on my parents' friendship with Edmond Martineau. Does that give you an idea of the way I feel about you?"

"Don't." She didn't want to hear any more. She was much too susceptible.

"I've barely thought of anything else but you since you walked out of my apartment," Rome told her. "I've picked up the telephone a hundred times to call you, but you looked so damned vulnerable when you begged me to leave you alone.''

''Why didn't you?'' Lexie moaned.

Rome ignored that. ''So, at the airport, when I had the chance to single you out, I did. I wanted you to see you were someone special to me, but I didn't even get a thank-you for it. I paid more attention to Claudine than was necessary hoping you would be jealous. And when I found you alone and I had a chance to see if being near each other was tearing you apart the way it was me, what happened? The first thing out of your mouth was politics—reporting.''

''What did you expect me to say?'' she cried.

''Anything but that,'' he retorted. ''So I gave you the information you were seeking, partly out of anger because you said it was the only reason you were there, partly out of selfishness because I wanted to show you again that you were special—and yes, partly because I wanted you to feel grateful to me. What did I receive in return? Your doubts. Your questions. You still didn't trust me.''

''Is it any wonder,'' Lexie protested, ''considering the kind of man you are?''

His mouth thinned in exasperation. ''We're back to my so-called philandering ways again, are we?''

''You just want another conquest.''

''Has it ever occurred to you that I might be looking for the right woman?''

''You'll never find her.''

''Maybe I have,'' he challenged.

''For men like you, there never is a right one, only right 'ones.' And I don't want to be part of a plurality in any man's life.''

"You haven't listened to anything I've said," Rome sighed, and let his hands settle on her shoulders to gently knead her taut muscles. "I want to see you again and go on seeing you. I don't know where you've got these ideas about me, but I want to show you they aren't true."

He was persuading her. His voice, his touch, his nearness were all working on her fragile defenses. "It wouldn't work," Lexie continued to hold out. "We're two different people. I don't even travel in the same social circle as you do."

"Snob," he mocked.

"Look at you," she persisted. "You're vichyssoise and I'm split-pea soup."

"Not split-pea soup," Rome smiled. "Spicy minestrone maybe, but not split pea. Besides, what is vichyssoise? Nothing but cold potato soup."

"You don't understand," argued Lexie.

"Why don't you explain it to me?" He glanced behind her to the tiny kitchen. "Do you have any coffee on?"

"No." She shook her head.

"Why don't you make some and we'll sit down and talk about the way we're different," he suggested, turning her around and giving her a little push toward the kitchen.

"It isn't a difference I can explain." Mechanically Lexie went about doing what she was told, filling the coffeepot with water and reaching for the coffee canister. "How can you explain feelings?" The canister was empty and she opened the cupboard door to get the new can of coffee on the top shelf. "They're there. They simply exist." Stretched on tiptoe she could barely reach the can with her finger-tips.

"I'll get it."

Rome was beside her, reaching over her head for the can, his few inches taller enabling him to reach it easily. As he lifted it down, his other hand slid in a more or less automatic caress down her spine to the small of her back, his touch infinitely familiar.

"My God!" he breathed in sharp anger. "You don't have any clothes on under that robe. Did you do that deliberately just to test me because you knew I gave you my word we would only talk?"

"Yes, I did it deliberately," Lexie flashed, stung by his censorious attack. "I find it much easier to take a bath without clothes. And of course, I expected you over here tonight!"

Rome pulled away from her, turning to the coffee can he had set on the counter. "Sometimes you can drive a man to the limits, Lexie," he muttered. "Go and get some clothes on while I fix the coffee."

"Remove temptation, is that what you mean? Why should I get dressed? Maybe I *should* use it as a test to see if you really can keep your promise."

By her very words, Lexie realized she had already started to give in to his persuasion. As he had accused before, she wanted to be talked into seeing him. Her weakness was frightening.

"Go," he ordered.

In the face of her discovery, Lexie obeyed. The cream linen pantsuit she had worn that day was still lying on her bed, along with a wildy figured brown and blue blouse. Stubbornly she avoided it, going into her closet to take an old pair of Levis off the hook and a shapeless gray T-shirt, to point out, with her choice of clothes, another of their differences.

"Where are the cups?" Rome asked when she returned.

"In the cupboard to your left." She walked into the kitchen.

His dark gaze glinted over her attire. "What are you trying to prove now, Lexie? That I'm too old for you?" he chuckled. "What is there? Eleven years between us?"

"Yes," she admitted.

"That hardly makes me old enough to be your father."

"I never suggested that you were," Lexie responded stiffly.

"I'm in love with you." His seriously gentle tone brought her head up. "I don't know if it was a case of love at first sight. Maybe it was the second, third or forth. But I love you, Lexie."

"No!" Her heart constricted painfully.

"What do I have to do to convince you that I'm sincere?" Rome questioned, his eyes intent and concerned. "Do you want me to get down on one knee and propose? I'm prepared to do that, too."

From his jacket pocket he took out a ring box and snapped it open. A diamond solitaire winked at Lexie, bright and sparkling, a rainbow of colors flashing in the overhead light. She gasped at the sight of it, then couldn't breathe at all, only stare.

"I assure you it's the real thing," he said with teasing gentleness. "I didn't buy it at the local dime store."

"I can see that." Her voice trembled.

"Give me your hand." Rome took the ring from the

box, but Lexie's hand remained rigidly at her side. "What's wrong, Lexie?" he demanded.

A thousand little needles were jabbing her heart. "I was just wondering how many others have tried it on," she choked.

His mouth tightened. "You can check with anyone you like—gossip columns, social register, my old girl friends, my parents. You'll find that I've never asked any woman to marry me. You're the first, Lexie. I want you to be my wife."

A sob tore from her throat at his moving words.

She turned away, jamming a fist against her mouth. "I want to believe you, Rome," she cried softly. "How I want to believe you!"

"I love you," Rome repeated, his hands returning to her shoulders. "Believe that," he ordered. "And I think you love me."

Lexie moved her head to the side but she didn't really deny it. "I. . . ." She didn't know what to say.

"Take the ring," he urged. "Wear it so that I'll know that you'll be mine. I won't press you into setting a wedding date. I'll wait as long as you want."

"I can't." She turned his arms tipping her head back to gaze at his face. "I can't take your ring, not until I'm sure."

"But you'll see me. You'll give me a chance to prove that I mean everything that I've said." They were statements that bordered on questions.

"Yes, I'll see you," Lexie agreed, guessing that her heart was probably lost forever to him anyway.

His arms crushed her to his chest as he buried his face in the silk tangle of her hair. "Come with me tomorrow," he commanded. "We can drive to Cape

Cod late in the afternoon. My parents have a cottage there. We can...."

"No!" Lexie strained away from his embrace. For one brief moment she had trusted him and already he was trying to take advantage of it.

He laughed softly and wouldn't let her go. "It isn't what you're thinking, Lexie. I'm not proposing a stolen weekend. My parents will be there to chaperone us. They're driving down tomorrow after Martineau and his daughter leave to relax after the hectic whirl of activities. It's all going to be perfectly respectable."

"Oh." Her voice was small as he swept aside her reason for objecting. "Your mother," Lexie hesitated, remembering the reaction at the airport. "I don't think she likes me."

"What makes you think that?" Rome lifted his head and frowned curiously.

"She knows who I am—the things I said about you in Shari's column."

"Yes," he agreed with a nod.

"She was the reason you came to see me at the newspaper. She was upset by them."

"She was worried for my sake," Rome admitted. "But believe me she doesn't dislike you."

"She gave me a very odd look at the airport," Lexie insisted.

"I think her woman's intuition has already warned her about the way I feel toward you. She was probably taking a good look at the woman who's going to be her future daughter-in-law." He smiled.

"Maybe." She qualified his statement.

"As far as I'm concerned there are no maybes about it," he stated.

"You say that now." In Lexie's mind, it was only a question of time before he became tired of her—a week, a month, a year, then years, but her joy was imprisoned by the knowledge that it would happen some day.

"You haven't given me your answer about tomorrow," Rome reminded her.

Lexie hesitated, then asked, "What time shall I be ready?"

Her heart did a somersault when he smiled at her. "Three o'clock." A smoldering light suddenly burned in his eyes and the smile faded from his bronzed features, as his gaze roamed possessively over her face. "Are you going to hold me to my promise, Lexie?"

She glanced at his well-shaped mouth, knowing the wondrous rapture that she would find in his kiss. She ached to feel it. But an inner demon of doubt drove her to deny both of them what they wanted.

"Yes, I am," she whispered.

Held so closely to him, Lexie felt the tensing of his muscles in protest. Yet Rome didn't argue as he slowly withdrew his arms from around her. The smile he gave her showed the strain of control.

"I'll be here at three tomorrow," he promised, and she nodded her head in agreement. Rome gave her another long look. "Good night, Lexie."

With clenched jaw he walked past her into the living room to the door. His hand was on the doorknob. In another second he would be gone.

"No!" Lexie cried.

Rome turned and she ran into his arms. Hungrily they kissed, the fire of their passionate love leaping into full flame. It would have raged into an inferno, but

Rome pulled her arms from around his neck and reluctantly dragged his mouth from hers.

"I want you, Lexie," he told her. She felt the tremors going through his muscular length and they were as violent as her own. "But I want you without doubts. I won't settle for less." It was a warning, accompanied by a hard sure kiss. "Tomorrow at three," he said, pushing her away from him and opening the door.

"I'll be waiting."

THE WEEKEND WITH ROME was more perfect than Lexie had dreamed it could be. After an initial bout of self-consciousness toward his parents, Lexie succumbed to their natural charm. They treated her as one of the family without ever making any allusion to her relationship with Rome.

They did practically everything as a group—boating, cooking, walking along the beach, although she and Rome did steal a few enchanted moments alone. Lexie found herself often covertly studying his parents, trying to ascertain if they were truly happy. There seemed to be affection between them, but she couldn't be sure.

Cape Cod, as always, was beautiful. On Lexie's previous visits she had been part of the thick stream of summer visitors, which had meant crowded hotels, chains of restaurants and endless traffic. With Rome she saw a different view.

The large but cozy Lockwood cottage was on a winding road in a quiet residential area where rambling roses grew along the lanes. There were miles of silver-gilt beaches and breezes carried the salt tang of the ocean. Time seemed to stand still on that leisurely

weekend, blessed by the magic of the sun and the sea—
and Rome's company

The following week she saw him often, lunching with
him one day, having dinner with him the next. She
realized he was courting her in an endearing old-
fashioned way. The moments were becoming more frequent when she wondered if she hadn't erred in her
initial judgment of him.

On Saturday they were to have spent the entire day
together until Mike called early in the morning with an
assignment for Lexie. It had promised not to take long,
so she had phoned Rome and postponed their outing
until late that morning.

With the assignment completed Lexie's steps were
eager as she left her parked car for her apartment. She
was to call Rome as soon as she was free. There would
be time to change her clothes and freshen her makeup
before he came.

Sweeping into the apartment on the airy cloud she
had been traveling on lately, she glimpsed her roommate's pale blond hair as she turned to close the door.
"Hi, Ginger! Why are you still here? Hasn't Bob called
yet?"

Miracle of miracles, she had even begun to look
kindly on Bob. Perhaps love did mellow a person,
Lexie thought as the door clicked shut.

"Not yet," Ginger answered.

"Hello, Sunshine," a third voice greeted Lexie.

When she turned she saw the man rising to meet her.
Tall and agelessly handsome, he smiled, an expression
his tanned features knew well. His red hair was a darker shade of auburn than her own golden-hued strands,
but the vivid blue of his eyes was the same color.

Her lips were dry, threatening to crack when she smiled. "Hello, dad," Lexie returned the greeting and forced herself to cross the room to receive the customary kiss and bear hug.

"It's good to see you again," Clark Templeton declared. "I've missed you."

Lexie smiled and avoided the expected similar response by asking, "Have you met my roommate?"

"Ginger?" Her father beamed at the blonde, who blushed under his look and Lexie knew her father had made another conquest. "I certainly have. How come you never mentioned in your letters that you were sharing your apartment with such a beautiful young lady? Those starlets in California would be envious if they saw her!"

Careful, Ginger, Lexie wanted to warn. *Don't listen to his lines.* But of course she couldn't. In the first place, Ginger wouldn't admit that she was attracted to Lexie's father, so what was the use?

Lexie disentangled herself from his arms but he kept hold of her hand. She knew they made a striking father-daughter combination. She had been told that often enough when she was growing up.

"This is really a surprise," she declared. "Why didn't you let me know you were coming?"

"It wouldn't have been a surprise, would it?" he reasoned with a chuckle.

"When did you arrive?"

"We caught a very early flight this morning."

"We?" Lexie repeated. "Did Mary-Anne come with you?"

There was only the slightest flicker of discomfort in his expression, but Clark Templeton covered it well.

"It must have been longer than I thought since I'd written you. Mary-Anne and I broke up months ago."

"I received a postcard from you a few weeks ago. You didn't mention Mary-Anne so I assumed things were still the same between you," she admitted, but she wasn't surprised by the news. "Who is the new 'we'?"

Her father didn't seem to notice the false brightness of her question. "Teresa Hall. She's part of the reason I flew here to see you. I want you to meet her, Sunshine. I've asked her to marry me and she's accepted."

"Well, congratulations," Lexie offered with brittle gaiety. "When's the lucky day?"

"We haven't set a date yet. I wanted you to meet her. After all, she is going to be your stepmother. You'll like her. I know you will."

"Of course," she agreed.

"I thought we could all have dinner tonight—you, me and Teresa. It will give the two of you a chance to get acquainted."

"I'd love to, dad, but I already have plans for tonight," Lexie explained with pretended regret.

"Are you going to a party or what?" He glanced from Lexie to Ginger, as if asking her roommate for the answer.

And what normal female could deny Clark Templeton what he wanted? Not Ginger. "Lexie has a date," she supplied the information.

"In that case, there's no problem," her father declared. "Bring your date along, too. We'll make it a foursome."

"I don't know," she stalled. "I'll have to ask him."

"You do that," he agreed. "I'd like to meet him and see the kind of young man you're dating."

"You'd like him, dad," Lexie said with a trace of irony in her voice. "He's a lot like you."

"Is he now?" He looked delighted, smiling broadly as if he had received the highest compliment. "I definitely want to meet him, then."

"I'll have to ask," she said again.

"I'm counting on you to come tonight and so is Teresa. I know you'll do your best to make it. In the meantime—" he reached in his pocket "I—want you to go and buy yourself a new dress—something blue to match your beautiful eyes." He pressed some bills into her palm.

"No, dad," Lexie tried to refuse.

"You take it," her father insisted. "A working girl can't always afford a new dress. Consider it your birthday present from me. Tonight is going to be a celebration and I want you to look your best!"

Her fingers curled around the money in her palm as she died a little inside. "Very well," she agreed.

"It's time I was going back to the hotel before Teresa thinks I've forgotten her," he joked.

After making arrangements with Lexie for her to call once she had talked to Rome, her father left with his usual charming disregard for the way he had disrupted her life.

"Honestly, Lexie, I don't see why you said you couldn't get along with your father!" Ginger declared. "He's an absolute doll! I wish my father was like him."

"No, you wouldn't," Lexie said dryly.

"Are you going to call Rome?" At Lexie's nod, Ginger asked, "Don't stay on the phone too long, will you? I haven't heard from Bob yet. If he doesn't call me pretty soon, I'm going over to his place and find out what's wrong.''

Lexie absently heard the closing of a bedroom door and turned to find Ginger had left the room. She stared at the money in her hand, then at the telephone.

CHAPTER NINE

AFTER TWO RINGS, the phone was answered and Lexie recognized Rome's voice on the other end of the line. "Hello, Rome. It's me, Lexie."

"That didn't take long." The warmth in his voice reached across the distance to her. "When do you want me to pick you up?"

She hesitated. "Something has come up."

"Not another assignment, I hope."

"No, it isn't that. My...my father has flown in from California." Her fingers curled into a fist, wadding the money in her hand.

"That's wonderful," Rome declared. "I'd like to meet him. Perhaps the three of us could have dinner together this evening."

"No. That is...." The first tear slipped from her lashes as the muscles in her throat constricted so tightly she couldn't speak.

"Lexie, what's wrong? Don't you want me to meet your father?" Rome sounded puzzled.

"No—I mean, yes." Lexie realized she wasn't making any sense.

"What's the matter?"

"You see, my father's getting married. He's brought his fiancée along," she explained.

"Are you upset by the idea of your father marrying? Is that it?" Rome questioned.

"Not really. Actually, my father invited you to dinner tonight, but since it's going to be in the way of a celebration, I wasn't sure if you'd want to come." At first she had wanted to keep the two men apart, but now she realized that she would be able to show Rome what she hadn't been able to explain in words.

"I intend to become part of your family, Lexie," he reminded her. "That includes your father and your prospective stepmother."

"Yes, of course," she agreed.

"Are you spending the afternoon with them or are our plans still on?"

Lexie wiped a tear from her lip. "Daddy wants me to buy a new dress for tonight." She didn't want to spend the rest of the day with Rome, so she clung to the excuse her father had unknowingly given her.

Rome caught the tremor in her voice. "You're upset," he accused. "The thought of your father getting married again does bother you. I'll come over and we'll talk about it."

"No, please," she denied. "It's all right."

"Lexie, are you sure?"

"I'd rather be alone this afternoon," she admitted. "I'll work it out."

"I'll be here all afternoon. If you want me, you will call?"

"Yes, I'll call," Lexie promised. "About dinner, we're to meet my father at his hotel at seven-thirty."

"I'll pick you up at seven."

"See you then, Rome. Bye."

Hanging up the phone Lexie slipped into her own

room and cried softly so her roommate wouldn't hear. She didn't want to make the explanations that nobody had ever understood. Later, the closing of the front door signaling Ginger's departure acted as floodgates to shut off the flow of tears. At last Lexie washed her face and splashed cold water on her swollen eyes.

With her father's money in hand, she went out and bought the new blue dress he had suggested. It was beautiful. The saleslady raved over the combination of Lexie's flame-colored hair and the midnight blue of the material. Lexie found no pleasure in it. She was fulfilling a duty as she had done so many times in the past. This time the color of the dress happened to match her mood, a deep dark blue.

The selection of the dress had taken a considerable amount of time and it was several hours before Lexie returned to the apartment to walk lethargically to her door. The evening stretched ominously before her like a long tunnel with no light at the end. Lexie walked on blindly because it was what she had to do.

Tucking the dress box under her arm, she unlocked the door and pushed it open. A red-eyed Ginger glanced up, sniffling once before resuming the task Lexie had interrupted. Lexie stared blankly at the suitcase sitting on the floor at Ginger's feet and the one her roommate was locking.

"I'm glad you're back, Lexie," Ginger declared in a voice that threatened to break into a sob at any moment. "I didn't want to leave without saying good-bye."

"Leave?" Lexie echoed.

"I'm going home." Ginger set the suitcase on the floor with others.

Lexie closed the door and leaned against it, bewildered and lost in the maze of events. "What's happened?" she breathed. "What do you mean?"

"When. . . when Bob didn't call me and I couldn't get any answer, I . . . went over to his place." Her roommate looked so forlorn, so shattered. "Oh, Lexie," she broke into a sob, "he had another girl with him!"

"Ginger, no," Lexie protested sympathetically, feeling the pain as if it was her own.

"Yes. He. . . he told me to get lost. You were right, Lexie," Ginger hiccuped a laugh. "Bob never loved me—he told me so. He only wanted. . . ." She left the rest unsaid, averting her head and letting her pale blond hair fall to the side in long curtain. "So I'm going home." Ginger tucked the hair behind her ear. "I never did like it here. Big cities just aren't for me. I only stayed because. . . . Well, anyway, I'm leaving."

"I'm. . . sorry," Lexie offered inadequately.

"You tried to warn me about Bob, but I wouldn't listen. I thought I knew it all." There was a wealth of bitterness in the declaration. "Anyway, I'm going home where I belong—where a guy still treats a girl with some respect." She seemed to get a grip on herself. "A cab is on its way to take me to the bus station. I called my parents and they're expecting me."

"Ginger, are you sure this is what you want to do?" Lexie questioned.

"Yes." The answer was decisive. Then Ginger faced her sudden recollection. "I forgot—there's an envelope in your bedroom with a letter telling you what happened because I wasn't sure I would see you before I left. My share of the rent is in it, too."

"You'd. . . ." Lexie started to protest.

"It's the least I could do. With the first of the month coming up, I didn't want to put you in a bind and you may not find someone right away that you'll want to share the apartment with. Of course—" Ginger gave her a brave teary smile "—the way things are going with you and Rome, you may not be wanting the apartment yourself."

"Don't be too sure," Lexie sighed. She knew she would soon be diving into the pool of misery and heartbreak that her roommate was drowning in.

"I don't care what you tell them at the newspaper on Monday," Ginger rushed on. "You can tell them the truth if you like. It doesn't matter." A horn tooted outside. "There's my cab."

Lexie set her dress box aside. "I'll help you with the luggage."

The phone was ringing when Lexie returned to the apartment from seeing Ginger off amidst tears and hugs and promises to write. It was Rome.

"Are you all right, Lexie?" he asked.

"Yes, I'm fine," she lied. "I was just going to get in the tub to get ready for tonight."

Rome didn't sound satisfied with her answer, but he accepted it. "I'll see you at seven."

He arrived a few minutes early, inspecting her closely, but Lexie was acting out a part she had rehearsed well, and her mask was firmly in place.

"You look a little pale," was the only fault he could find.

"Nerves," Lexie smiled away the reason. "I'm a little anxious about this evening." She left Rome to draw his own conclusion from that.

Her father was waiting in the hotel lobby when they

arrived. One look at the woman with him and Lexie's suspicion was confirmed. Teresa Hall was Lexie's age, a vivacious, tawny-haired creature with a gorgeous California tan.

Lexie was prepared for it. Her father's girl friends had been getting younger as she got older. As the introductions were made she stole a glance at Rome. If he was surprised by the relative youth of her father's fiancée, he didn't show it.

Clark Templeton had chosen the restaurant that Lexie had taken Rome to that first time. "I was told it was one of the best in the city," he said.

"It is," Rome agreed and sent Lexie a twinkling look of remembrance, but when she said nothing, neither did he.

"I didn't have any difficulty getting reservations," her father said as if he felt he should have. "But I did call early," he continued by way of explanation.

Rome suggested that they all ride in his car—even though her father had rented one—explaining that he was more familiar with the city than Clark. Her father readily agreed.

On the drive to the restaurant, Lexie felt sick at the quiet murmur of voices from the backseat where her father and his fiancée sat. Rome reached over and held her hand but she found no comfort in his touch.

Following the other couple into the restaurant, Lexie saw the maître d'hotel's glance fall first on her father and Teresa, then to Rome. When it touched on her red hair, he smiled, remembering her from the previous time.

"A reservation for four for Templeton," The maître d'hotel spoke before her father had an opportunity.

"Yes." Clark Templeton was plainly stunned. "How did you know?"

"Lexie and I have been here before," Rome explained, "As a matter of fact, on our very first date."

"What a coincidence!" her father declared. "It's almost prophetic that I chose this place, isn't it?"

Remembering how disastrous the previous time had been, Lexie thought that it probably was, but she offered no comment. They were shown to their table and drinks were ordered. Although she said little, Lexie made a show of entering into the spirit of the evening, smiling and drinking to the toasts her father proposed.

During the meal Rome made a reference to their previous weekend's visit to Cape Cod. Her father smiled and set a teasing glance at Lexie.

"Did you go boating?" he asked.

"Yes." It was natural to return his smile. "And without incident, too."

"Clark loves boats," Teresa spoke up, sending an adoring look at the man whose ring she wore. "He has a cruiser tied up at a local marina and we spend almost every weekend out on the water."

Lexie had only to close her eyes to picture her father in his white ducks and a yachting cap on his head. He cut a dashing figure, she knew, with his face to the salt spray and the sun glaring on the ocean waves.

Clark reached for his fiancée's hand, carrying her fingertips to his lips. "Teresa loves the water as much as I do. It's one of the many things we have in common," he declared. "We both love to snorkel and go deep-sea fishing. Two weeks ago she landed a shark. I'm having it mounted for her to hang in our den. She's quite a girl, my Mary-Anne."

"Her name is Teresa," Lexie corrected quietly, and smiled at the girl so near her own age. "You'll have to forgive my father; he has trouble with names. He remembers them, but he puts them with the wrong faces. I've learned to answer to anything!"

Neither her father nor Teresa seemed embarrassed by his error, although Lexie felt Rome's quizzical look. It had obviously happened before.

"It's all right," Teresa explained with loving smile at her fiancé. "I know I've had a lot of competition, but all those others are in the past now."

Lexie thought, *Honey, you ain't seen nothin' yet,* but she just smiled and murmured some suitable response. She had wanted Rome to meet her father and understand her feelings. But when had understanding ever changed anything?

"Talking about boating," her father continued brightly, "we had a terrible time with Lexie when she was a child. She used to get seasick at the sight of water. Fortunately, she outgrew it." He laughed. "Remember the time Angela took you to Disneyland and you got sick on the Jungle Cruise?"

"That was Beth," she corrected, and felt a nauseous lump rising in her throat. "Angela took me to the museums."

"Was it Angela? I thought it was Doreen," he said, frowning.

"No, Doreen liked sports," Lexie reminded him, and took a sip of her wine to try to wash down the lump in her throat.

"Is that right?" Her father sounded skeptical. "I always thought.... Oh, well, it doesn't matter. As Teresa said, it's all in the past." *But the past has a way of repeating itself,* Lexie thought. "But it certainly was a wonderful day when Lexie stopped being seasick," he reiterated.

A comment seemed to be expected from Rome and he made it. "I'm sure it was." As if sensing the need to change the subject he picked up the bottle of hock and offered, "More wine?"

But Lexie had had enough—enough wine, enough talk, enough of everything. All that remained was a desperate need to escape. There had been nothing to gain by going through this evening. She realized that now. She had lost all that mattered to her before it started.

But it was difficult to lose something that had never been hers, and Rome had never been hers, even if she had pretended it was possible for a little while. She knew better now. Her father's visit had been opportune, because she had needed to be reminded of that.

Lexie pushed her chair from the table and rose, trying to mask her haste with an air of nonchalance. "Would you excuse me, please?" she asked brightly, knowing they would all presume she was going to the powder room.

Rome half rose from his chair, his eyes sharp and questioning, but she touched his shoulder lightly as if to assure him that everything was all right. She paused at the maître d'hotel's desk, glancing back to make sure she couldn't be seen from the table.

"Yes, Miss Templeton? What can I do for you?" the maître d'hotel inquired soliticiously.

"Would you call me a cab, please?" she requested.

"A cab, miss?" He raised an eyebrow, his glance straying in the direction of her table.

"Yes, please," Lexie repeated. She guessed his curiosity and hurried to allay it. "After I've left, would you take a message to Mr. Lockwood?"

"Of course."

"Tell him that I wasn't feeling well. I have a headache and have taken a cab home and for him not to worry. Tonight's dinner is something of a celebration for the others," she explained, "and I don't want to inconvenience them or cut short their evening."

"Of course, Miss Templeton, I understand." He nodded. "I will have a cab brought around to the door in a few moments."

"Thank you." And she fervently hoped it would only be a few moments.

True to his word, he returned in a very short time to tell her a taxi was waiting out front. After giving the driver her address, Lexie leaned back in the seat and closed her eyes against the stabbing rush of pain.

It seemed that they had barely left the restaurant when the cab pulled up to the curb in front of her apartment. Lexie fumbled in a blind haze through her bag for the fare, paid him, and hurried to her empty apartment.

Inside she turned on a light and walked no farther than the lumpy cushions of the sofa. She stared dry eyed at the ceiling. The mask that had been in place all evening was abandoned. Her features bore the pitched, whitened lines of strain and the agony of hopeless love. There was a grim consolation that she hadn't accepted Rome's engagement ring and was thus spared the torture of returning it.

Her hearing caught the sound of someone in the hallway, but it made no impression on her consciousness.

The world could have come to an end and Lexie wouldn't have cared. It would have been a relief of sorts not to have to go on with the day-to-day monotony of living.

There was an imperative knock on her door that tensed her muscles. "Lexie?" Rome called her name and knocked again. She didn't move. "Lexie?" The pounding on the door hammered at her head. "Lexie, I know you're in there. Answer me!"

His commanding voice prodded her into speaking. "Go away!"

The doorknob rattled and Lexie was glad she had had the forethought to lock it when she came in. Her fingers were curled into the cushion, clutching it tightly as if to prevent herself from going to the door.

"Lexie, unlock this door," Rome ordered.

"Please, just go away and leave me alone," she moaned.

"I'm not going anywhere until I see you. Now open this door!"

"If you don't leave, I'll call the police, I swear!" Lexie sobbed. "I don't want to see you. Just go away and leave me alone!"

There was silence, the knocking ended, then there was the sound of footsteps echoing down the hallway. Lexie had won. She rolled face down onto the couch and began crying; racking sobs heaved her slender body. What heartbreak it had cost to deny him!

Lexie knew she would have to do it again because she knew Rome would make another attempt to see her. Eventually she would have to explain that she wouldn't see him anymore. And this time she would be steadfast in her decision.

The clink of metal and the rattle of the doorknob pierced the foglike pain of her consciousness. She gulped back the sobs and lifted her head. Copper curls clung to her tear-moistened cheeks and she pushed them away in time to see the door open and Rome walk in.

"How..." she mumbled, and struggled upright, a disheveled mess.

"I told you I wasn't leaving until I saw for myself that you were all right," he told her, and turned back to the door.

Her blurred vision had a glimpse of a figure behind him. Confused, Lexie saw the flash of something bright in his hand outstretched to the other person. It took her a full second to recognize that it was a key ring.

"Thank you, Mrs. McNulty," said Rome. "I'm sorry to have troubled you like this."

Mrs. McNulty, her landlady from downstairs. She had let him in with her passkey. Lexie's paindulled mind realized that that was how he'd got through the locked door.

"'Tis no trouble," the landlady insisted.

That charm of his, her heart cried. It had even worked its magic on Mrs. McNulty. Lexie never would have thought that her strict landlady would have let a man into one of her apartments rented to single girl.

"Go away!" Lexie cried, and started forward. "I don't want to see you!"

So desperate was she to have Rome leave that she didn't pay attention to where she was going. Her knee bumped the wooden coffee table and she nearly fell over it. Before she could recover on her own Rome was there, his hands imprisoning her arms, holding her upright and steadying her.

"I'm sorry," he offered over his shoulder, the apology directed to the landlady. "I know Miss Templeton doesn't want you to see her like this. I'm afraid she's had too much to drink tonight."

"I'm not drunk!" Lexie denied, knowing she barely tasted her wine.

She tried to twist out of his hold, but his strength was too much. With the slightest exertion of pressure he caused her to stagger forward against his chest, reinforcing his claim of her inebriated state.

Mrs. McNulty clicked her tongue in reproof. "That's what my late husband used to say, too, God rest his soul. He never drew a sober breath in his life," she sighed.

Lexie sobbed at the comment. The woman was convinced and Lexie was too overwrought to try to correct the impression. She lowered her head and tried to ignore the exquisite pressure of Rome's touch.

"There's some coffee in the kitchen," Rome said, still addressing his remarks to her landlady. "I'll get some of that down her. Perhaps that will help."

"It's the best thing," the woman nodded.

"If she needs assistance getting to bed may I call on you, Mrs. McNulty?" he asked. In effect, he was dismissing the woman from the apartment.

"I'll be right downstairs if you need me," she promised and moved toward the door.

"Thank you."

And Lexie laughed with faint hysteria at the way he had wound another woman around his finger, pulling her strings and directing her to do his bidding. The door closed and he set her firmly down on the couch. As he walked away Lexie turned to see where he was going. In the kitchen he put the coffee on to heat.

"I don't need any coffee. I am not drunk," Lexie insisted. Did he think she was?

"I know that." He took a cup from the cupboard. "But you could use some strong hot coffee just the same."

Lexie didn't argue about such a trival thing. She needed to conserve her strength for what was to come. Her hopes of putting off this discussion to some future time weren't to be realized.

CHAPTER TEN

HER EYES AND CHEEKS were dried when Rome entered the living room with the cup of hot coffee. There was a determined set to her chin as she glanced up at him, towering beside the couch, and accepted the cup from his hand.

"Why did you come here?" It was more of a bitter protest than a question.

"Did you expect me to believe that excuse about a headache?" Rome countered.

"It's real." Her temples were throbbing, a thousand snare drums beating in her head.

"Real or imagined, you surely didn't think I'd let you run away like that without an explanation," he persisted.

"Do you need one?" Lexie stared at the shining black surface of the liquid in the cup, wishing she could sink beneath it into oblivion. "Wasn't it obvious?"

"I can imagine how you must have felt when you met your father's fiancée," He seemed to answer the question carefully. "I know it's probably difficult to adjust to the idea of your father remarrying. Evidently he failed to mention the fact that his prospective bride was no older than you."

Lexie lifted her gaze to stare, unable to believe the words she was hearing. His handsome face was grim, a troubled darkness in his eyes lit by a spark of compassion.

"Running out like that didn't solve anything, Lexie," Rome said, tempering his criticism by a gentle voice. "You still have to face the fact that he's going to marry her."

"No," she mocked.

"You're just making it more difficult," he reasoned. "I want to help you but you have to let me."

"Didn't you listen to anything that was said tonight?" Lexie accused him in disbelief.

Rome frowned, not following her question. "What do you mean?"

"Teresa isn't the first girl friend my father has had who could pass for my sister," she declared in agitation. "Angela, Beth, Doreen, Cynthia, Mary-Anne— he's practically gone through the alphabet. He's all the way up to the T's!"

"Girl friends, yes, but this one he's marrying," he reminded her. "There is a difference."

"Is there? Do you think this is something different?" taunted Lexie. "Since my mother died, I've had three stepmothers. My father finally got wise and stopped marrying before he was financially destroyed by all the alimony payments. I've lost track of how many times he's been engaged. He always insists each time that this is the right one. The sad part is I think he really believes it. Of course the poor girl never is the right one. Give him a year and my father will be accidentally calling some new girl by Teresa's name."

"You aren't making any sense." Impatience edged Rome's voice. "Drink your coffee."

"I'm making a lot of sense." Absently she took an

obedient sip and felt the hot liquid burn down her throat. "You just don't want to understand."

"If it isn't because of your father or his engagement, then why are you so upset?" Rome demanded.

"Don't you see?" she pleaded. "You and my father are just alike. You're both handsome and exceptionally charming men. Look at the way you just persuaded Mrs. McNulty to let you into my apartment!"

"And you think—" he began angrily.

"I don't think, I know," Lexie interrupted. "Ever since my mother died, there's been a steady stream of beautiful women in my father's life. At first when he brought one of them home and announced that so-and-so was going to be my new stepmother, I used to try to like her, to be friends with her. But they never stayed around long enough. Someone else always took their place. I always had to compete with somebody for my father's attention. I can still remember hearing my mother cry because he didn't come home until late at night."

Rome sat down on the couch beside her, resting his elbows on his knees and clasping his hands in front of them. He stared for a silent minute at his intertwining fingers, his jaw hard, his mouth grimly straight.

"Why didn't you tell me all this before?" He slid her a sidelook.

"Would it have done any good?" she whispered, her heart aching. "Would it have made any difference?"

"At least I would have understood why you were so reluctant to trust me," Rome stated, and let his mouth twist into a smile. "But you didn't trust me enough to tell me."

"Sometimes words aren't convincing. You wouldn't

have believed me. You had to be shown." Her voice was barely above a murmur. "You and my father are two of a kind." She saw him start to deny it and rushed on. "I've seen what happens when you walk into a room. I don't think there's a woman born that can say no to you and it's the same with my father. Women are putty in your hands. When you get tired of playing with one, you pick up another."

"You aren't putty to me, you're a woman. I don't want to play with you, I want to love you," Rome declared with convincing steadiness.

"I love you, Rome," Lexie admitted. "I don't even have the excuse that I didn't know what I was doing. My eyes were open. I knew what kind of a man you were, but it will never work, because I won't sit home and cry for you the way my mother cried for my father and I won't compete with other women for you. I'm tired of competing. I only know that I couldn't live my life with you never being secure in your love."

"I've given you my love, Lexie, offered you my ring and my name, asked you to spend the rest of your life with me." His gaze searched her face. "What more can I say or do to make you believe me? If the positions were reversed, how would you prove you loved me?"

"I . . . I don't know," she answered.

"Neither do I. Do you want me to buy a desert island? Maybe I should throw acid on my face."

"No!" Lexie cried out at the thought.

"Then tell me what to do, Lexie, because I'm not letting you go. Not now that I've found you." As if to enforce his statement, Rome took the cup from her hands and held them. "I'm only half alive unless I'm with you or unless I know that you're near. How do I convince you that I am not like your father?''

"It's no use." Her heart splintered as his persuasive words tore her apart. "Rome, I've seen you look at other woman when you were with me, admiring them—"

"Yes, I look at beautiful woman. I admire them the way I would a painting. That doesn't mean I want them to be my wife or that I want to make love to them. If you see a good-looking man, do you pretend he doesn't exist?" he challenged.

"I. . . ." Lexie fumbled for an answer and couldn't find one.

"Don't expect more from me than you do from yourself. I'm not a saint, Lexie," Rome warned.

"I don't expect you to be a saint," she said.

"Don't you?" For an instant he was taunting her with bitterness. "What do you expect of me?"

Lexie trembled, "I just want you to love me." Her eyes were blue luminous saucers, mute and appealing.

His expression softened as his hand cupped her face in a caress. "I do. I've asked for the chance to spend the rest of my life proving it, Lexie."

Her lashes fluttered down, letting the warmth of his touch steal over her skin. When he exerted a faint pressure she let herself be drawn into his arms. Lightly he kissed her temple and the wing of her brow.

"I can't begin to explain why your father is the way he is," Rome told her. "It would probably take a psychiatrist to figure it out. If, as you say, he's made a habit of seeing young beautiful women, maybe he's afraid of growing old. Maybe he hasn't learned yet that it's a privilege few of us ever get to enjoy. But, Lexie,

I'm not like your father. For me there's only you. Every other woman can vanish from the face of the earth as far as I'm concerned.''

Lexie lifted her head a few inches in order to see his face. His look was so earnest, so determined, so compelling. There was so much strength of character in his male features. And the burning flame of love in his eyes simply could not be faked.

"I believe you," she whispered, and it was the sweet glorious truth.

His hand was at the back of her neck tangling in her hair and drawing her upward to his mouth. The moaning sigh that escaped from her lips an instant before they felt the crush of his kiss carried with it the last doubts, banishing them forever from her mind. Her arms slid inside his jacket, curving around his waist to spread her hands over the sinewy muscles of his back.

With unrestrained joy she answered the urgency of his kiss, the blood singing through her veins with the wildly happy song of her love. Rome twisted her onto his lap, touching her, caressing her, needing the reassurance of her responses.

As his head bent to explore the ecstatically pulsing vein in her throat, Lexie murmured, "You'll have to teach me how to trust, Rome. It's something I didn't learn very well when I was growing up.''

"There are a few other areas of your education that have been sadly neglected, too," he added, his mouth moving against the silken texture of her skin.

"Such as?" She smiled as an assortment of lessons ran through her mind.

"Such as learning when to stop talking." And he let his mouth silence her for the time being.

Lexie didn't mind. It was enough to be in his arms and knowing that he truly loved her. The erratic beat of his heart beneath her hand was the most beautiful sound she had ever heard—perhaps second only to his low voice saying "I love you." He was life, and from him flowed her vitality.

"My ring—" Rome teased her lips with his "—you will wear it?"

"Yes," she agreed in a voice choked by the depth of her emotion.

"I've been carrying it with me," he said smiling, "just in case you changed your mind."

Her hand was trembling as he slipped the ring on her finger and kissed it, then the sensitive hollow of her palm before sealing a final vow against her lips. It was a searing fire of possession that leapt through her, flaming and holy in its desire.

"Do you suppose your landlady thinks I've gone?" Rome pushed aside the material of her dress to nibble a pale, golden shoulder bone.

"She's bound to have noticed how quiet it is up here," Lexie admitted, and shivered at the sensual caress. "She probably thinks I've passed out."

"It was the only excuse I could think of to persuade her to let me into your apartment," Rome smiled, and a series of kisses traced the outline of her lips.

"I wonder if she'll come up to check," she mused, and let her fingertips explore the chiseled contours of his face.

"I doubt it."

"If she does my lease will be canceled for sure." But Lexie didn't care.

It would take an atom bomb to get her out of Rome's

arms now. This was where she belonged. This was home. It always had been, only she had been too frightened to admit it.

"Then you can move into my apartment," he said.

"Will you do all the cooking and laundry?" she teased.

"No, my little feminist, you will."

"We'll share," she compromised.

"Maybe I should knock something over to get Mrs. McNulty to come up," Rome suggested. "Then she can throw you out. We can elope and you can start living with me and end all this frustration."

"It won't be necessary to go to such lengths," Lexie laughed softly. "I'll marry you whenever you say."

"Tomorrow," he stated.

"Mm." She drew away to give him a considering look. "That might be soon enough."

"I love you, Lexie," he declared in a sharply indrawn breath.

She pressed her lips to his. "I love you, too, Rome," she said against them.

The kiss soon deepened with drugging ardency. The caress of his hands became more demanding and evocative. Her arms wound around his neck as she strained to eliminate the physical limitations of the embrace. Rome stiffened and tried to draw back, shuddering with his effort at control.

"When will your roommate be home?" he asked thickly.

"She won't." Lexie pulled him back.

"What do you mean?" His lips hovered above hers.

"She's left for good, moved out," she explained.

"You mean...." Rome began.

"Yes," Lexie breathed.

With a stifled groan he covered her mouth and pressed her backward onto the cushions. The time for words had come to an end.

**For the millions who can't read
Give the Gift of Literacy**

One out of five adults in North America
cannot read or write well enough
to fill out a job application
or understand the directions on a bottle of medicine.

**You can change all this by joining the fight
against illiteracy.**

For more information write to:
Contact, Box 81826, Lincoln, Neb. 68501
In the United States, call toll free: 800-228-3225

**The only degree you need
is a degree of caring**

"This ad made possible with the cooperation of the Coalition for Literacy and the Ad Council."
Give the Gift of Literacy Campaign is a project of the book and periodical industry,
in partnership with Telephone Pioneers of America.

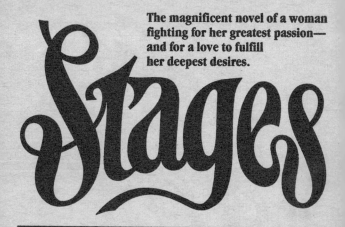
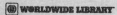